The Rook Circle

Volume 1

Jef Rouner & Dori Hartley

To: Candace

Thank you for all
the wonderful support.
It makes things
much better.

This is a work of fiction. All characters and events portrayed in this novel are fictitious and are products of the author's imagination and any resemblance to actual events, or locales or persons, living or dead are entirely coincidental.

Disclaimer: The following stories contain some extreme subject matter such as sexual violence. Though I have hopefully handled the subject in as tasteful and respectful a way as possible, to those with sensitivities I would like to include a trigger warning and an apology. Stay strong, Readers With One E. You're all beautiful.

This is for Lynda. She knows why.

-JR

Everything I do, great or small, is dedicated to my daughter Alex.

-DH

60 Degrees: I Failed the Balloons

I never really gave much thought to balloons since I entered this nebulous haze that the law calls adulthood until my daughter was born. Who has time for little latex helium prisons? Even the fancy ones… you know, the licensed characters of a prodigious size that you buy to show that you really, really care? It's a lot of nothing. A mindless ritual that we all adhere to for reasons that we don't really examine.

It's killing us, too. Did you know that? Our vain whimsy is destroying us. The world is running out of helium at an alarming rate, and we need it to chill MRI magnets and make LCD screens and a whole mess of other technologies that you had no idea were beholden to the stuff you inhale to make funny voices. It's the lifeblood of an age of wonders, and we're bleeding it out to make Dora the Explorer float at a four-year-old's birthday party.

We're mad. At least, I hope it's all of us. Not that I want a mad world. I'm just scared of being alone.

Where was I?… balloons. Right.

So, as a child, my daughter loves balloons. I can see why. She's a small thing tethered way closer to the ground than I. What child doesn't see the graceful float of a balloon and not feel inspired? Another fun fact: a balloon overcomes the same force that holds a distant planet-like body, such as Pluto, millions of miles away in a tight orbit around the sun. Imagine that - strength to move worlds can be overcome with seven dollars, a tank and a vague likeness to Scooby Doo. I think kids feel the upset and the insanity that is such a thing and cling to it in their own desperate way. Here is a colorful, floating symbol of everything being rewritten beyond human understanding.

Reality on fire. Kids love that.

So I buy her balloons, but she's still a child. She leaves them behind for other playthings. All that remains are the spheroids that glide through my house on the currents of the air conditioner. They're utterly silent, tethered to plastic clips that leave them traveling at head height. More than once I have found myself up late at night hammering words into a computer only to see them float past the corner of my eye like ghosts. They stalk me in the dark when I rise to use the bathroom. They're hovering above me when I wake between nightmares.

In spite of the scares, I'm not so old and rusted that I don't see the power of such things. Life is symbols, after all. You, me and all of the archetypes that we carry around in the little bags that are our souls, form a collection of tropes and props, pulled as needed to give the world the drama and the story it requires to keep on spinning. You didn't think gravity did it alone, did you? It can't even knock a balloon back down to Earth and you expect it to make the dawn come up?

Balloons leak. They go from majestic, perfect bodies to crawling, bouncing cripples. If you wait long enough, they'll actively crawl across the floor on the barest of dropped breaths, gamely dreaming of ascension. It's entropy in the purest form. A fascinating yet terrifying process to witness.

I don't much care to see it myself.

So, in the gap between my daughter's fixations with the balloons she begs me to buy her and their gasping death on my cat-marked carpet, I set them free. I wait until the house is small and dark and quiet and there are as few demons in my head as possible. You live for the dark between the seconds of a clock's tick, when there are no stories being told around you but your own. They're cold moments, but all real freedom is cold.

I go outside and stare into the sky above me. For a second, it's me and a balloon just tied together and hoping and praying and dreaming. Then I let it go and follow it until it passes beyond my sight. George Carlin once said that there was a room in West Heaven where every balloon you have ever lost waits for you. Third door on the left, or something like that. Such a nice thought.

Sometimes, though… I'm not fast enough. Life is hectic and busy and strange. You wake up, and you realize that the balloon you'd promised ascension to is barely bearing the weight of its own string. On those nights, I'm short and edgy until my family is in bed. The second my last wishes for sweet dreams are uttered, I race outside and hurl the balloon into the wind. There are times when it finds the strength. The Texas wind grabs it and helps it into the sky like a Boy Scout helping an old lady cross the street.

But other times, it's for nothing. The wind serves only to carry it over a fence and into the street. One car after another rips the balloon into bits until its promise is ground into the asphalt and shredded beyond hope.

It's funny how we can fail even the simplest things in our care. It makes you wonder how you ever get through the day. I can't even maintain the minor illusion of a balloon set free on a consistent basis. Illusions, stories are so fragile. Like glass.

And, like glass, if you do not tread with care, those stories will cut you and bleed you and maybe even kill you. Ahead of me are dead dreams and broken glass and heartbreak and needles and medications untaken and just the barest glimpse of hope on the wind driven forth by the beating of a rook's wing. It's time, my friends, to walk the circle.

Underbite

"So you see, my old friend and enemy, your kind can never-"

Thwock.

"Hope to stand against the sons and daughters of the eternal nigh-"

Thwock!

"Et-eternal night. In our blood is the history of atrocity and death itse-"

THWOCK!

"Would you mind terribly not doing that anymore? It's very rude."

The little man handcuffed to the chair in front of the vampire slowly lowered his head, which, moments ago, he had been banging as hard as he could into the metal post that the chair was secured to. He looked at the vampire with withering disdain.

"The agony of choice is especially apropos when you're choosing between agonies," said the little man with a very slight Minnesotan accent. "In this case, I can either endure this ridiculous monologue, feeling my brain atrophy slowly from the ears in, or I can go for the comparatively quick route and hopefully knock myself into a coma before you get to the part about humans as cattle."

The vampire was honestly somewhat at a loss. He expected his triumph over Van Helsing, THE Van Helsing, to be an epic battle culminating in a grand finale. Frankly, none of it was living up to his standards, and he wondered if he maybe "accidentally" let Van Helsing go, there might be a chase involved that would be more satisfying. He hoped the man would at least change his clothes.

Whitney Van Helsing, short, pudgy, and with thinning brown hair corkscrewed off into improbable tufts, had chosen to meet the vampire in a Hawaiian shirt, checkered golf pants... and crocs. There was no dashing, romantic old-war costume, no doctor's bag full of stakes, holy water, or high-tech, ultraviolet-emitting bullets. His entire arsenal against the lords of shadow consisted of a cell phone several generations of technology in the past, a ring of keys, and a wallet with a rewards cards for a local frozen yogurt store. He needed one more hole-punch to get something called a Swirlzel Flavor Bucket free of charge.

At the bottom of the card: "Participation may vary".

Surely, Whitney's ancestor had not confronted Dracula in crocs, though the vampire couldn't recall footwear ever being specifically mentioned in any of the surviving texts. Maybe he would ask other vampires on the chat forums afterward under a different name so it wouldn't look silly.

What kind of name was "Whitney" anyway?

"It was my mother's maiden name," said the little man out loud, and the vampire jumped slightly.

"The stories are true!" said the vampire. "Your line does hold mysterious secrets born of strange alchemies. You can read thoughts, but such a trifling power will not stop me from ending the meddling of your family with our race."

"I can't read thoughts, you pinhead," said Van Helsing. The vampire could almost see the words in the air, the exasperation of the little man was so thick and rich. "How many times do you think I've done this bit? Dozens? Hundreds? Heck, I don't even know anymore. I don't need telepathy to follow the incredibly linear thoughts in your head, an,d I don't have to be Sherlock Holmes to track your disappointed glances at my clothes and shoes."

"Well," the vampire said, "It's insulting!"

"It's comfortable!" replied Van Helsing. "Why do you think hunters and nurses basically work in their pajamas? It's because they have important things to be getting on with, and they want a comfortable outfit to do it in. Same thing for me."

This was just not going very well at all. The vampire crossed the darkened warehouse to an elegant baroque set-up lit with candles in the corner. This part was at least perfect. It was a grand mixture of horrors! The rusting machinery around him was great for instilling terror in modern minds while off in this bedroom, he could play Victorian dark gentleman surrounded by antiques, brass, and mirrors. He thought the juxtaposition clever, and his use of the word "juxtaposition" cleverer still.

He didn't feel clever now, though, and he watched Van Helsing in a mirror with his back turned to the little man. Now there is a good-looking monster, the vampire thought, admiring himself. All silk and velvet with a nice cravat just under his thin, bone-white face. Black clothes, of course, but with some purple highlights to hint at regality. Long, tousled hair. Aquiline nose. He'd look great in a movie. His smile died when he

focused on the eyes of Van Helsing looking at him. In spite of his yokel, non-threatening appearance, there was indeed something unsettling in that gaze, and the vampire was sure that the little man had followed his vain thoughts step by step.

The vampire strode back to Whitney Van Helsing and stood in front of him.

"You know that I could kill you as easily as I could kill a fly, correct?" asked the vampire.

"So can crossing the street," replied Van Helsing sounding bored.

"I mean that I'm going to kill you," said the vampire, hissing the words through his fangs for emphasis.

"Something surely will eventually," replied Van Helsing. "This makes you about as special as Tuesday."

"I CAN TEACH YOU THE MEANING OF PAIN UNTIL IT BECOMES AS YOUR GOD! UNTIL YOU WORSHIP IT IN FEAR AND HOPE OF ITS MERCY!" thundered the vampire.

Van Helsing blinked.

"Do you know," he said. "That was actually a pretty good little turn of phrase there. Not overly original, but well-worded, I thought. You should write it down. Work on it a bit, and maybe it will grow into something."

"Uh," stammered the vampire. "Thank you?"

"You're welcome, not that it changes anything," Whitney went on. "Cancer can teach you the same thing, and it's just a bunch of mindless cells that have forgotten to grow right. I saw my poor niece

14

Hilary go down like that. Inch by inch. Screaming the whole time as her body rotted from the inside."

Whitney fell silent, his mind obviously somewhere else. The vampire had the weirdest urge to fill the awkward silence with his condolences for Van Helsing's loss. The moment dragged on.

"Anyway," said Van Helsing coming back to himself, "my point is that, yes, you can do mean, horrible things to my soft, fleshy self that, yes, I would dearly appreciate you not doing and would probably scream throughout the process until death became a blessing. I absolutely believe you can and would do these things, sure, but death comes to us all, and you're not especially better at it than humans or nature. Really, you're not."

"That's where you're wrong, hunter," declared the vampire grandly. "The nosferatu are the absolute masters of the killing arts. We paint portraits in cessation, compose whole symphonies of screams. We are the artistic elite of Death himself, and that is why we will always rule over you pathetic huma- God dammit, cut that out!"

THWOCK! THWOCK!

The vampire was really in a mess now. He'd just stamped his foot like a child. This wasn't how it was supposed to go. He knew Van Helsing was hunting him and had slyly led him back to this lair where there were plenty of shadows to hide in, waiting for the perfect moment to strike.

He'd easily knocked the little man to his knees, dazing him long enough to drag him to the chair he'd already outfitted with restraints.

15

He couldn't believe how simple it had been. He'd outwitted the legendary scion of the hunter line almost effortlessly, and now he would have the opportunity to tell every vampire he knew that they could rest each day in peace knowing that Van Helsing's legacy was over. He couldn't wait to upload pictures of Whitney's broken, bled-dry body to the Facebook page! Terms of standards be damned!

Now he was glad he hadn't had time to set up a video recorder because, even though his prisoner was physically helpless, the vampire couldn't even seem to threaten him right.

"What's your name, son?" asked Van Helsing. He sounded tired.

"I am called Melkarth," said the vampire.

"I'm sure you are to your face," said Van Helsing. "I don't suppose you actually are a member of the Tyrian royal family or an ancient Phoenician or anything like that?"

"No. It's the name I chose when I was born again to darkness," said the vampire.

"Well, my father wanted to keep the Old Testament thing going with me," said Van Helsing. "It's tradition, you understand? My brother is Noah, but mom's family also had this tradition of using maiden names as first names as a way to keep the past connected. I've got an Aunt Parker, a cousin named Cartwright, and even poor Hillary was her mother's maiden name. So after Noah was born, my dad gave in and here I sit before you, Whitney Midian Van Helsing. At your service."

"Melkarth," bowed the vampire. "At yours."

"No, no," said Van Helsing. "That won't do at all. Look, son, think about the great names of history and how they unsettle people even today. Adolf Hitler. Rasputin. Attila the Hun. Calling him that was basically the same thing as calling me Whitney of the Gopher State. When you really think about it, I mean. Heck, Rasputin's name is actually very close to the Russian word for 'pervert', did you know that?

"Yet, if you named a kid Rasputin today, they would just assume that you intended him to become a sorcerer. That's the power of a legacy. You don't pick a name and try to fit it. You take the name you were given and you make it fit you. It's one of the reasons I wouldn't be caught dead in whatever silly formal wear you thought I was going to show up in. I'll ask again. What is your name, son? What did your mother call you?"

The vampire thought about it. What did it matter? The little man would be dead soon anyway.

"Stephen," said the vampire. "My name was Stephen Cory Davis."

"I don't know why you'd let that go," said Van Helsing. "Stephen is a fine name. It means 'a crown'. Don't know what Cory means, though. Sorry.

"Now, Stephen," continued the little man with his steady gaze, "I want you to undo these handcuffs. I want to formally challenge you to a duel. You'd like that, wouldn't you?"

"It would hardly be a fight, old man," sneered Stephen. "I have ten times your strength and speed. Age cannot touch me, nor

17

poisons. I heal almost instantly, and I have other powers unique even among vampires."

"That all sounds frightfully impressive," said Van Helsing kindly. "Clearly there isn't anything I can do to stand against such power, woefully weak and unprepared as I am. But at least you could let an old man die on his feet. Die bravely facing the darkness he was, in the end, completely ineffectual against just as the day is helpless against the fall of night."

"Yes," said the vampire. Finally, they were getting somewhere. Should he get out his phone and try to video the confrontation? No, it never picked up enough light in here to do a good job of it. "I owe you, our ancient enemy, that respect at least."

With that, he moved like lightning and released Van Helsing so fast he looked like he hadn't moved at all. That always unnerved humans, the blurry speed. The little man just stood and rubbed his wrists.

"Make your peace with your God now, Whitney Van Helsing!" screamed Stephen, baring his fangs and leaping for the man. Next thing he knew, the vampire had fallen after tangling himself in the chair rushing through the space Van Helsing had just vacated with surprising agility. His head came into contact with the metal pole hard enough to make its own impressive THWOCK, sending his vision blurry. Van Helsing stood above him, offering his hand to the vampire.

"Good lord," said the little man. "That looked like it hurt. Here, sit up slowly, and let me look at your head."

Stephen complied, vague memories of his human father, a doctor, caring for him when he fell off his bike swirled in his confused and sore noggin. Van Helsing prodded the bump on the vampire's head, looking a little concerned when Stephen yelped, and then peered deep into Stephen's eyes.

"Vampires aren't immune to concussions," said Van Helsing. "In fact, if that undead healing factor kicks in too hard too soon, it can actually make the effects a human would either succumb to or heal from permanent in a vampire brain. Sometimes you hear of vampires going mad and walking into the sun. I've autopsied a few of them, and they had frontal lobes as smooth as a ninety-year-old Alzheimer's patient. Severe chronic post-concussion syndrome, that's what it was."

Stephen was terrified. What if that was true? Would he live as an immortal invalid? Oh God, Alzheimer's... a vampire with Alzheimer's or something like that. He'd never even thought about such a thing. It wasn't supposed to touch an immortal like himself. He felt sick.

Van Helsing guided the young vampire over to the candle-lit baroque corner of the warehouse and sat him on the bed. Stephen was told that he was under no circumstances allowed to lie down, and that the little man would check on him again in about half an hour as that would tell whether or not the concussion was settling on its own or being made worse by his vampiric physiology.

Van Helsing sat in a nearby armchair. In the candlelight, with his hands steepled in front of him, the little man no longer looked laughable. Now he looked, well, dangerous.

"Listen, Stephen," he said after a minute had passed. "I think that we ought to talk a bit more about some of your world assumptions. If I am going to die here, I'd really rather not it be at the hands of some rookie who will saunter off from the kill thinking he's an all-powerful fiend of darkness and then gets his head cut off celebrating by standing up in a convertible as he goes under a low bridge. It would be most embarrassing to explain to dear old grandpa Abraham."

"Okay," said Stephen weakly. He wasn't sure if it was the head injury or the tone of the hunter that was the cause of his sudden meekness.

"For instance," the hunter went on, "you simply must relieve yourself of this raging superiority complex that is so typical with vampires. I understand the reasoning behind it. I truly do. As you said, you have physical abilities far beyond those of individual man. You're strong, fast, a few of you can even fly, though it doesn't take more than a few collisions with pissed off ducks before they get over that particular gift. You feel invincible, but do you feel that way now, Stephen?"

"No," said the vampire, just barely managing to bite off the word "sir" before it passed his lips. "I don't feel invincible, but I'm still better than human."

"Alright," said Van Helsing. "How? You're physically a better specimen than me, but so is any rich, young, human man with access to martial arts teachers, good meals, personal trainers, top-notch health care, and the like. I'm willing to bet a great many of those young men are not currently sitting on a bed trying not to soil themselves in terror because they may soon be inflicted with permanent mental illness they can't get fixed. Your abilities are only a matter of degree, not really more so than those born to privilege have always lorded over those not. Clearly those advantages are not proof enough. What else have you got?"

The vampire was silent. He really didn't want to say the thing he was thinking because he needed Van Helsing to check him again. Melkarth had once spent a month stalking old folks' homes, watching Alzheimer's patients either tucked tightly in at night to keep them still or wandering the halls looking for things they couldn't remember. He'd laughed then, laughed the laugh of someone that's never known pain and can see its execution only as a comedy show. Dear God, he was so scared. He didn't think those confused faces that gasped as he walked out of the darkness to feed were funny now.

"Vampires are masters of the kill," said Stephen quietly. "That's the thing. We hunt you. We stalk you. We feed on you at will and almost nothing you can do can stop us. I mean, that's the food chain isn't it? The lion and the lamb and all that. You're the masters of cattle. We're the masters of you."

Van Helsing looked hard at the vampire, his expression unreadable and unblinking.

"Although, yeah, I do suppose humans kill vampires more than cattle kill humans," he said, trying to make a little joke.

"Actually, you're wrong about that, if it makes you feel better," said the little man. "Cows kill twenty times more people every year than sharks do. The mighty shark… beaten by the animal that becomes a Whopper every day. What do you make of that? The number gets even worse when you start taking into account things like mad cow disease, colon cancer from too much red meat, and environmental damage done from raising cattle in the first place. You're underestimating the cow by a pretty significant factor.

"That's your problem. You're a predator, not a creator or a thinker, and you're considering the world only in the terms of your next meal. You're hungry. You eat. You're successful. Game. Set. Match. That's all you're comparing it to.

"But think about this: how often do you kill, Stephen? If you don't mind me asking. Something like three a week? Six tops if it's the holidays?"

The vampire nodded.

"Let's go with four a week for convenience. So with those numbers, it would come out to a little more than two hundred a year. That means it would take you almost seven years to equal the man who made a bad call at the helm of the *Titanic*, and twice that to accomplish what a handful of religious fanatics did with two airplanes and a couple of buildings in New York City. You alone don't even measure up to human incompetence and the basest level of misplaced rage.

"That's just you, though, of course. Not the whole of the vampire race. Would you like to guess how many vampires there are in the world?"

"I don't know," admitted Stephen.

"What's the largest number you've ever seen in a room?" asked Van Helsing.

"Probably thirty," said Stephen.

"The largest recorded gathering of vampires was actually in Reno about fifty years ago," Van Helsing went on picking up the threads of the story. "It was a combination political summit, bloody orgy, and meet and greet. The guest list had about fifteen hundred names on it. They tried it again in Munich twenty years later and barely broke seven hundred. Vampires are getting scarcer every year, even if from what I can tell the birth rates aren't actually going down much. Your people make as many new vampires as they ever seemed to, but less and less of them live any significant time. It's not me doing all of that. They just tend to get killed more.

"I estimate that there are less than thirty-five hundred vampires total in the world right now. Your lot is in bigger danger of extinction than the polar bears. If we use you as an example, that tells us the entire vampire race kills 700,000 people a year. Congratulations. Adolf Hitler did the same thing in five months less time, and he was just one man. Start throwing in total deaths resulting from Hitler's actions in World War II, the upset in the

Middle East when displaced Jews established Israel, Stalin's purges, the Cold War, and you realize that when it comes to death and atrocity, you are nothing next to humanity."

"Well, we feed on you..." countered the vampire.

"So does athlete's foot!" shouted the little man with unexpected force. "You're not getting it. It's not black and white. A bull shark on land is a hunk of flopping meat. A bull shark in the water is more than a match for man, vampire, and a whole host of other things you haven't even had nightmares about yet. You define yourself by your ability to kill and feed, and you fail even in that to outdo your prey. More people kill themselves than are killed by vampires."

By this point, Van Helsing was out of his chair, pacing back and forth with nervous energy. Stephen was truly frightened now. Not of his own condition, not even of the man before him, who he now fully appreciated was the product of the finest occult extermination techniques ever devised. He was afraid that Van Helsing was right.

"That's not what they told me," said Stephen quietly. Van Helsing stopped.

"What did you say, son? Speak up, please."

"That's not what they told me when I was, you know, turned," said Stephen. "It was all this big party. Fenris and Delilah and Kahn brought me up out of the grave and told me that I never had to fear anything again, that I was the greatest creature ever to walk in shadows. Vampires were lords of everything humanity feared, and you? You were just dumb animals, at best, to be pitied and definitely to be relieved of your ignorant lives."

Stephen looked up and saw that his words here had done more to dishearten Van Helsing than beating him up and handcuffing him. In fact, he'd never seen a person so tired. Van Helsing returned to his chair.

"I'm going to try this one last thing with you, son," said Van Helsing. "Then after that, I'm going to finish my diagnosis, and you're going to do whatever you do. I'm an old man, and it's late, and this is my final attempt to try and make you see the world as it is, okay? You listening?"

"Yes, sir," he said, this time not even bothering to pretend he didn't respect this strange, terrible man.

"Look around you. All around you is the end product of those same dumb animals. This machinery was developed from the collective learning of humans over the course of two centuries. The cool air from the air conditioning, the architecture that holds the roof up, the electricity that powers your cell phone, the cell phone itself. Vampires created none of it. I've never seen a single bit of vampire-engineered technology in my life. Neither had my father. Or his father.

"Or even all this stuff in the corner you like. The gilded mirror, the tasteful bedspread, that sculpture over there which, incidentally, I know came from a craft store down the street because they sell it in every one of those stores in the chain. It doesn't matter. Whether it's a Rembrandt or a hunk of bronze, mass-produced garbage, it's art, and humans are the ones making it.

"Where are the vampire painters? Hmm? Where are the scientists that could use a century of study to create marvels? Where are the vainglorious vampire fashion designers who could dream up outfits for you to wear? They don't exist. They just don't. You get promised immortality, are gifted with privilege beyond measure, and you don't do a single thing with it except steal whatever you like from your prey and pretend it's your due.

"What did you want to be when you grew up, Stephen?" Van Helsing asked.

"I wanted to be a dentist," the vampire answered tonelessly, and the little man burst into unexpected laughter.

"Oh, that is rich!" said Van Helsing. "No, no. Don't be offended. Please. I'm sorry. I really am. It's a more than a worthy dream. It's just... a vampire dentist. A fang expert. See? Right there. You let a dream die when, frankly, your people could use someone with knowledge around the mouth. There's more than a few of you who have resorted to needles and scalpels to feed when some rather interesting parasites set up shop in their gums.

"I wanted to be a farmer when I was a kid. You're positively glamorous compared to me. Still, that's what I wanted to do. I wanted to grow things in the ground and ride a tractor. I used to go on and on about it as a child. Can't imagine how my dad stood it knowing that the whole 'Chosen One' speech was coming one day. I'm right glad I don't have to break the news to my nephews. Noah was the breeder in our family. He was the one who... made things. Grew them. Tended to them."

Van Helsing leaned forward and clasped his hands in front of him.

"So here we are, Stephen. Both of us wanted to do something with our lives. I wanted to feed people, and you wanted to make sure that they had teeth to eat with. Now you're part of a bloodsucking race of parasites that does nothing but consume and never produces a single thing of value to the world so eaten up with their own gluttony as they are. Sure, tell yourself that you're better than your dinner, but you might want to think about what you owe that dinner when you wear the clothes they made, drive the cars they built on the roads they constructed and enjoy the luxury that you're cutting them off from.

"And me? I'm not better than you. I hope that makes all this a little easier to take. I don't make anything. Oh, I save people's lives. There's no arguing that, but as I pointed out, you're not really all that big on the scale of things that need fixing in the world. I just do this because no one else knows how as well as I do. It's all I know. I'm a hunter like you, but when I kill a vampire, no one gets a meal. It's pest control, and I really fucking don't want to do it anymore. I'm not too old to still start that farm somewhere."

The timer went off quietly on Van Helsing's phone. The thirty minutes was up. He got up and shined the light of his camera phone's flash into Stephen's pupils, then had the young vampire follow his finger through several movements.

"You're fine," said the little man. "No concussion, but I think you should take it easy for a few days. Another injury could do some

28

serious damage to places I can't explore without surgery or an x-ray. The healing factor is working according to speed as far as I can tell."

"So, what happens now?" asked Stephen. Van Helsing shrugged.

"It's up to you. I'm awfully sick of this job, son, and there are two ways out of it that I see. The first is that you kill me, and one of my poor nephews or distant cousins begins the whole process of continuing the work ridding the night of Dracula's bequest all over again. Nothing changes except the color of the uniforms at halftime.

"The second is that you get a clue. Do something with your unlife and encourage others to do the same. Maybe if you weren't skulking like cockroaches you wouldn't get killed like cockroaches. Maybe there's a chance for cohabitation. At the very least, take some night courses and learn how to weave a basket or something. It's a start. The day you begin making something instead of just taking something is the day you grow up. Age doesn't matter. I once killed a vampire that was two thousand years old and who couldn't replaster a wall with a hole in it. What a waste. A hundred of him wasn't worth the fry cook I found him feeding on, no matter how shiny his shoes were."

Van Helsing stood up and began to walk away.

"That fry cook was in school, you know? I found out later. She was studying robotics. Probably so she'd never have to flip burgers again. Isn't that charming? Even the people actually making something sometimes create to destroy themselves."

Stephen sat on the edge of the bed long after the door to the warehouse slammed shut. He was thinking very hard about what Van Helsing said. What was he accomplishing with his life in the end? Kill, eat, repeat. Even throwing sex in there didn't really offer anything new. Man, he'd been calling humans cattle for years, but humans didn't need cows to procreate, and, except for a very small statistical amount of them, they didn't seek them out and seduce them before drinking blood from their necks.

When you put it that way, his life sounded really sad and pathetic.

The little man was right. Time to do something about it! There was a whole world out there full of things that he could do and contribute to. Night classes, right. They always had those brochures lying out. He could learn Spanish or web design or something.

Stephen pulled out his phone, logged onto the vampire secret Facebook group and began typing.

"Hey, you guys. I just had the best idea…"

***

Two days later, Whitney Van Helsing was sitting on the bus, quietly reading the newspaper. Buried three pages back was a story about a suspected arson in a nearby warehouse filled with strangely elegant antiques among the disused machinery. One body had been recovered and was believed to be the corpse of a slumbering vagrant who had been trapped in the building and unable to get out. No suspects were known at this time, nor did there appear to be any motive for the fire.

30

The victim was unidentified. His fingerprints had been burnt off, and he didn't match any known dental records in the database. One forensic expert considered that strange as the subject had an extremely healthy set of teeth, minus the canines, which had been removed with surgical precision.

"That sort of thing would likely have been noteworthy enough to be fairly well known a good ways around," said the expert to the paper. "Hopefully someone will come forward and help identify this poor man."

Van Helsing put down his paper and picked up his phone. He located the website of the Academy of Laser Dentistry because it was the coolest sounding thing in his Google search, and donated five hundred dollars to the Dr. Eugene M. Seidner Scholarship Program intended to promote the advancement of dental laser education and clinical research by helping dental students pay for schooling.

He signed the donation Melkarth.

The little old man looked out the window of the bus into the windows of all the banks, stores, hospitals, and more. Not a single green thing grew here, he thought, but it's something.

It's a start.

A Senseless Eating Machine

Every day for the past decade, Reggie Roberts brought children to shark infested waters. He loved their screams of terror, and the deadly silence that followed. It was the best job that he ever had.

Ringing the bells of his miniature steam engine, Reggie pulled a line of ten small carriages behind him, filled to the brim with families eager to ride the Shark Train. Along the paneled sides of the carriages a story of undersea marvels was painted. Giant squids battled sperm whales to the death, and sailors from a galleon looked on in terror as they mistook the enormous oarfish for the legendary sea serpent.

He could have easily recorded his announcements on the train, but he liked the more personal touch of narrating the ride as they chugged around the grounds.

"Before we enter the world-famous Houston Maritime Adventure Shark Tunnel look to your left, and you'll see another apex predator of the ocean," said Reggie. The passengers did as they were told and gasped at the enormous creature sunning itself on the rocky beach next to a large pool. "We call this big boy Ouroboros, and he is named after an ancient dragon said to be so large that he could circle the world and bite his own tail. Boris, as we playfully call him, isn't quite that big, but there are reports of saltwater crocodiles just like him reaching over twenty feet, and they may live for as long as a century.

"Boris comes to us from Australia, where saltwater crocs thrive as the largest living reptiles. They are incredibly dangerous, killing at least one human a year. Even though our handlers have taken care of Boris since he was a baby, they must always be extremely cautious around him because the species is fiercely and aggressively territorial. Don't worry about us, though, folks. We're perfectly safe up here."

The giant crocodile followed the train with eyes that were the size of silver dollars and never seemed to blink. Large reptiles deeply unsettle humans. It's their stillness, like a machine on standby that is somehow still aware and regarding you. The pace was just unnerving and awed by Boris as people always were, they were generally glad to be past him.

Through the tangles of trees, Reggie continued to guide his train, happily pulling on the whistle just for fun. Kids loved that. Once past the crocodile's lair, there wasn't much animal-watching, aside from a pond of flamingos and a lonely giant tortoise named after Reggie's aunt Maisy. The real adventure was coming up.

Ahead loomed what looked like an old fort, but that was just stucco and red paint. In reality, it was a renovated lumber storage facility, but here at the Maritime Adventure it was Maison Rouge, the hideout of the Gulf Coast pirate lord Jean Lafitte.

The train bustled through the building, and the passengers gaped around them as early 19th century Galveston was represented on the walls. Wax mannequins of Lafitte's pirate crew drank grog and pawed serving girls while the man himself sat on a throne at the top of a pile of stolen gold. Reggie told tales of the Gulf Coast corsair and grinned at what came next.

Suddenly the lights dimmed except for a low, blue glow ahead. In the dark it was hard to tell the grade of the track, and the Shark Train picked up speed as it suddenly dove downward underneath speakers that played the terrible and too-often familiar sounds of a powerful hurricane. Reggie himself had recorded the wind and rain during Hurricane Ike, just for the proper touch of bringing back the fear of the devastating storm. Between the speed of the ride and the thunder and lightning effects, many of the people in the train began to cry out.

Reggie pulled a lever, and the Shark Train slid to a stop as the wail of the brakes echoed in the heavy silence that descended. The train was underwater now, in a large glass tunnel that wound through an enormous aquarium. Off to the left the wall resembled a sunken pirate ship, while above them the water was dappled with the sunlight of the world above. It was a faint, weak light that made you feel like the surface was miles away, a nice touch that Reggie accomplished with tinted sunroofs to weaken the harsh Texas sun.

There were sharks everywhere. All around them, silently gliding in and out of the wrecked ship, past the glass walls, and most alarming, over their heads.

The timing here was why Reggie never bothered to record his message. You had to feel for the perfect moment right before the crowd got over the fright of the descent and started talking among themselves over what they saw. Get it just right, and you've got them in the palm of your hands.

"Ladies and gentlemen, above and around us is roughly half a million gallons of saltwater," said Reggie, turning around in his engineer seat to drape an arm nonchalantly over the cab of the train. His laid back appearance and easy, deep voice was weirdly homey and welcoming in the strange environment.

"As you might also have noticed, above and around us are also sharks. Lots of sharks. In fact, the Houston Maritime Adventure boasts one of the largest exhibits of the most dangerous sharks known to man, some of which were previously thought too dangerous to keep in captivity.

"The two large, stout sharks you see swimming around are bull sharks, one of the most deadly sharks in the world. They tend to inhabit the shallow coastal waters, be extremely aggressive, and are believed responsible for more attacks on humans than any other species. In fact, the Jersey Shore shark attacks of 1916 that inspired the movie *Jaws* are now thought to be the work of a bull shark, not a great white. These predators can grow as long as eleven feet, and have the unique ability to swim miles up freshwater rivers like the Mississippi."

Reggie continued to list the other sharks seen in the exhibit, but this stage of the scare was over. He noticed a little blond boy tracking the larger of the two bull sharks, utterly deaf to Reggie's descriptions of the nurse, lemon, and sandbar sharks. Even highlighting the fearsome, demon-mouthed sand tiger shark got the beast no more than a glance as soon as Reggie explained that the shark was relatively harmless with no confirmed attacks on man.

Finishing his description, Reggie started the train chugging forward again slowly. The tunnel curved around to the right for a ways in order to give it enough momentum to climb back up the hill to level ground. As the train passed through the tunnel, Reggie began his last set-up.

"Some sharks are thought to be utterly incapable of being held in captivity," he mused. "We ourselves tried to add a great white shark to the exhibit some months ago, but she managed to actually escape into Buffalo Bayou. Don't worry, folks. Great white sharks can't live in freshwater, so I'm sure that our girl is no longer any threat to Houston."

He smiled to himself as the train came out once again into the sunlight. On his left was a pool of water cleverly disguised to look like it did indeed connect to the bayou in the distance even though it was actually little more than a couple of feet deep and held less water than your average above ground swimming pool. The train continued to curve to the right, and so most people tended to look that direction. Reggie counted on that.

In the pool was a massive, animatronic great white shark head. It was state of the art, at least as state of the art as cheap jump scares got. Reggie waited. There was a switch that tripped just as the engine passed the head, and when it did, the shark would leap out of the water, brandishing its teeth while water jets made the appropriate bang to make folks jump. Even for repeat riders of the train, it got them every time.

The engine passed, and the water jets blew. Reggie, intent on guiding the train around the curve, hit his line without looking back.

"Oh no! It's the great white! We'd better call the aquarium staff to come collect it immediately!"

He smiled until he realized that the screaming wasn't stopping. Looking back over his shoulder, Reggie's face went from chocolate brown to ashen grey.

The small blond boy he'd noticed earlier had somehow gotten his arm trapped up to the elbow in the metal teeth of the shark. Blood shot in every direction as arteries and veins were severed both by the bite and by him being pulled from the still-moving train despite the grip of his father. Now, the animatronic was beginning to reset, descending back into the water as the pneumatics let out so as to be hidden from view to terrify the next set of customers.

If the boy didn't bleed to death, he would drown.

It seemed to take hours, but couldn't have been more than thirty seconds, all told. Reggie slammed the brakes, and people shook from the unexpected stop. Quick as he could, he turned the train into reverse, hoping to re-trip the switch and get the shark's mouth open again. He wasn't entirely sure if it would work going backward.

Luck was with him, though. He saw the relay go on and slammed the brakes again to bring the train to a stop. The shark leaped, carrying the boy up and forward with brutal

mechanic momentum but the jaws opened and he fell helplessly into the reddening water. Stuck on the activation circuit, the robot was on a continuous loop of attack, snapping and biting at the train as jets banged and spray went everywhere. People panicked, fleeing through the trees to the right, away from the shark, just as Reggie saw security running up, alerted by the screams.

The training that Reggie had received long ago in the navy as a special operations combat medic kicked in, and he sprinted from his seat, engineer hat falling off his salt and pepper hair. The poor boy, who couldn't be more than ten, was already in shock. Above him, the massive robot continued its mindless snapping while the boy cried and cowered. Reggie reached him just as the boy's father did, having been thrown out of the train in the second maneuver. Reggie scooped the boy out of the shallow water with the father right behind him.

Finally out of range of the attraction, Reggie set the scared and very badly hurt boy down.

"I'm medically trained," said Reggie to the boy's father. "Security is going to be busy making sure none of those people blunder into a dangerous exhibit. Run up the tracks, and enter the first building on your left. Tell them to call an ambulance and that we are at stage five. Did you get that? Stage five!"

"What the fuck is going on here," screamed the man. "I don't—"

"I said RUN!" screamed Reggie. "Building. Ambulance. Stage five. Come right back and help me. Move."

The man moved. "I'll be back, Micah," he called as he ran.

Reggie looked down at the boy. Unwilling to take his eyes off him for a single second, he grasped his uninjured wrist in one hand so he could monitor his pulse and stretched himself to feel for the first aid kit in the engine. It wasn't uncommon for people to receive minor injuries in the park. They stuck their hands out of the moving train and banged them on tree trunks or walls, and Maisy the tortoise could be kind of nippy if the long-necked turtle wasn't in the mood to be prodded at through the fence of her enclosure.

Nothing like this had ever occurred at Maritime Adventure, though. This was gruesome and even Reggie's kit, much more complete than your average kit out of habit leftover from the navy, wasn't going to do much but stabilize the kid before the ambulance got here. That's what stage five meant. It was code for serious injury or fatality.

He pulled the boy's arm out as gently as he could and constantly repeated a litany of "You're alright, you're okay," but there was still a small scream from the kid regardless. The wound was just above the elbow joint, four deep slashes that were probably a result of the bite mechanism opening and closing. The teeth of the robot weren't particularly sharp. Certainly they lacked the razor-like quality of a real shark tooth, but they were still pointy and powered by a pneumatic motor that could have lifted a tractor trailer.

He got out disinfectant and sterile cotton swabs to sanitize the wound. God knows what sort of bacteria clung to those teeth. The water in the pool was deliberately left a little murky in order to better hide the shark. A staph infection was a definite possibility.

Reggie slipped on a tourniquet, careful not to tighten it to the point of cutting off the circulation. Once the blood flow was slowed and the bites cleaned, Reggie got a better look at the arm itself. One bite went all the way to the bone, and Reggie could see the wrenching he'd gotten being hauled out of the train had resulted in a bad spiral fracture with some minor crushing. Just then, the boy's father came back.

"Is he going to be OK?" the father asked.

"So far, so good," said Reggie. "What's your name and his, sir?"

"I'm Craig Ochoa," said the man. "This is Micah."

"OK, Micah," said Reggie. "It looks like you're definitely going to need stitches, but we're going to wait until the ambulance gets here first because I managed to get the bleeding slowed down pretty well. Can you wiggle your fingers for me?"

Micah did so with a wince, but his movements were weak and barely noticeable. The arm was probably going to be fine in the long run, but Reggie would leave that to the hospital to decide.

"Any problem getting an ambulance, Mr. Ochoa?"

"They said one should be here in a few minutes."

"Well, that's aces. Micah's not in any danger now, but what happened?"

Craig Ochoa was not a big man. He was perfectly medium-sized and right at this moment he looked lost and tired. His t-shirt was

41

matted with mud, water, and sweat, and Reggie was willing to bet he could barely see out of the fogged up eyeglasses on his face. When he removed his baseball cap to wipe his brow, it revealed long, straggly, and thinning brown hair.

Boy must take after his mom, thought Reggie randomly.

"I don't know what happened," said Craig. "We've been here a dozen times. He always loves the Shark Train, and he was looking right at the spot where the great white jumps out. He was even pointing at the shark when it happened, and that's how his arm got stuck."

Reggie looked at the man curiously, then down at the boy. The shark had a range of around four feet. It was twice that distance to the train tracks. A chimpanzee could have tried to stick his arm in the mouth deliberately and wouldn't be able to make that distance, let alone a small boy.

Yet here they were. Reggie himself had seen Micah being dragged back, and now that he thought about it, the shark did seem to be remarkably closer to the train than ever before when it was biting and snapping at the people while the switch was stuck.

"I'm sorry I didn't keep my arm inside the train," said the kid through tears.

"Hey, little man," soothed Reggie. "Don't you worry about that. You didn't do anything wrong, you hear? I think you're very brave, and we're going to get you fixed right up. I don't know what's up with that old shark, but you can bet we're going to take a look just the second we get you taken care of."

He gave the boy a big goofy grin, and Micah returned it uneasily. In the distance, they heard ambulance sirens. Reggie turned to Craig.

"Stay here," he said. "I'm going to bring them in. Keep him still in this position, and don't move him. I'm pretty sure his arm is broken, and we want to leave it to the EMTs to set it."

Reggie reached into his engineer overalls front vest pocket and pulled out a business card.

"Once things are settled at the hospital, give me a call," he told Craig. "I'll get someone to bring your car out to you with your refunds and some incident paperwork that will include our insurance information. Give that to the doctors and we'll pay the bill. If you need us to bring you some food or anything else as well, just tell me."

Reggie stood up.

"Our lawyer's information will be in the packet, too, if necessary."

Craig nodded. Reggie reached down and patted his shoulder.

"He's going to be alright," said Reggie. "I've patched up people bitten by actual great whites back when I was working for Uncle Sam. Your boy is going to pull through like a champ."

Reggie began to walk toward the front of the park. As he did, he spotted the EMTs coming toward him. He pointed out the way to Craig and Micah and then trudged in the opposite direction, starting to feel every one of his 55 years as the adrenaline turned him back into an old man. Up ahead was a bench in the shade where he could wait to make sure they got out the gate with no problems.

He'd been sitting quietly for just a minute when a high-pitched voice said, "Hi, Reggie!" Reggie groaned internally.

Sitting next to him was Keesha Leicht of the Houston Post. He'd forgotten she'd asked for passes today for her and her boyfriend so she could do a small piece interviewing his two divers that would swim in the coral reef tanks dressed as mermaids. The tails cost him thousands, and he was hoping for a nice bit of publicity from Leicht's bubbly enthusiasm for such things.

"Hey there, Keesha," said Reggie tiredly. "How was the mermaid show?"

Keesha glanced at him with blue chip diamond eyes, and any hope that this was going to not be in the news quickly faded after one look. Oh well, better her than most. If he got this out of the way right now, the story might just be retellings of whatever he said right here.

"The mermaid show was great," said Keesha. "It was really well done, and the girls gave some lovely quotes. I wonder, though, what's with all the screaming, and why are you covered in blood?"

Reggie looked down and saw that his uniform was indeed smeared with Micah's blood. The EMTs chose that moment to come around the bend with the boy, his father trailing behind. Keesha and Reggie silently watched them go past and get into the ambulance to drive away. Lastly, out of the jungle came Keesha's boyfriend,

Aaron, and to Reggie's disappointment, he was clearly selecting pictures that he'd taken on his phone.

"You know that shark is still jumping around like it's on robo-meth, right?" he told Reggie.

"Ah, crap! I forgot," said Reggie and he started walking back. Keesha and Aaron followed.

"I had Aaron go around through the tunnel to see what was happening while I waited for someone in charge to get a quote from," said Keesha brightly, flipping on her recorder app. Damn it, thought Reggie, this was not good. He sighed.

"A boy stuck his arm out of the train and somehow got it caught in the jaws of the shark," he told her. "I dispensed medical aid and called the ambulance. The shark's been there since we opened in '08, and nothing like this has ever happened before."

"Dispensed aid?" asked Keesha. "Are you trained? What's the injury like?"

He briefly recounted the accident, taking every word like slippery stones used to cross a stream.

"Any idea why it happened?" she prodded.

"Keesha, this was like fifteen minutes ago. I haven't even gotten the train back to the station or made sure all the passengers have been rounded up safely yet. We will do a diagnostics on the machine the second I get the damned thing switched off and into the work area."

"If the shark isn't not off now, then why is it suddenly so quiet?" said Aaron unexpectedly.

The trio stopped. Around them, they heard the sounds of the city and the park, but that was all. Reggie didn't like it.

At the pool, the shark's head was half exposed over the water, just enough to see the eyes and snout. The large black orbs reflected Reggie as he walked up alongside the pool. The hot, humid air stank of oil and fish and blood and sweat.

"Doesn't seem to be moving now," said Keesha. "Does it, like, run-down? Like clockwork?"

"It shouldn't," said Reggie. "It's plugged into the main power grid, same as everything else. Maybe the train shifted off the switch, or maybe it's got a cycle limit. I haven't looked at the programming in years."

Reggie waded around behind the shark and into the bushes along the back of the Shark Tunnel. In a small shed there he found the main power cable to the robot, unlocked the panel with his master key, and deactivated it. Just to be absolutely sure, he also physically removed the plug. He'd bring in his tech Gina tomorrow when she got back from visiting her mom in Maine.

Aaron was snapping pictures when Reggie came back out and waded through the pool. The shark didn't seem any different for having been shut down. You'd have thought the pneumatics would have let out and submerged the head again, but it was still in the same position. A bloodstain coated the nose and dripped slowly into the water with an irritatingly mechanical rhythm.

"All aboard, kids," said Reggie, swinging up into his seat. Aaron and Keesha climbed into the first car behind him. "I'll take you back to the front and give you a prepared statement."

Just to be sure, Reggie reversed most of the way back into the tunnel exit before chugging forward on the train's normal course. He found himself cringing as they passed the trip switch, but the shark sat motionless and dead just as it should have.

***

It was nearly midnight, and Reggie was still in his office. Though it was easy to mistake him as an unskilled laborer with his job driving a kiddie train, Reggie Roberts was, in fact, the owner of the small theme park. After he'd left the navy he'd gotten a job as a freelance consultant for high-end aquarium folks, and that had led to the city offering him start-up money to build the park as part of an expanded tourism initiative. Most of what you saw around the grounds was secondhand from defunct theme parks and a few impressive private collections. There were a lot of rich folks in Houston, and they often had the strangest things lurking in their storage sheds that they refused to throw away. That's where the train had come from, and most people were happy to have him haul the stuff off if it meant having their names on a brick somewhere.

Secondhand or not, Reggie was a meticulous and patient man that oversaw the repainting and reconstruction of every single aspect of his new venture. His two roller coasters were repainted every year and lovingly maintained without a single accident report on either. His midway had a perfect inspection record and his food stands

47

almost as good. Playground equipment was clean and free from graffiti, and all of it re-purposed was nautical themes by one hundred percent local artists and sculptors.

It was a complete success, invested in by the city every year in loans and always paid back with interest by Reggie, thanks to the constant influx of visitors. The cobbled-together nature of the park gave it a unique personality, but now Reggie wondered if it might be responsible for hurting that poor kid. Had he overlooked something in one of his castoffs?

After all the passengers had been rounded up, the train was closed and parked in the storage shed overlooking Boris' enclosure. Everyone was given refunds and the doors to the shark tunnel locked. Reggie got on the phone to Gina, who informed him she'd be in from the airport around 11 p.m. assuming an on-time flight and would come right over rather than wait until tomorrow.

In the meantime, Reggie watched security footage with a frown until he heard her distinctive four-time knock.

Gina cleaned up nice, but rarely bothered. She certainly didn't have time for that nonsense after a plane ride and in the midst of an emergency. Jeans, *Pokemon* shirt, and her impressively long brown hair shot through with grey rolled up into a bun so tight you could bounce a quarter off of it, that was her style. She and Reggie had an easy and warm professional friendship, but she was a terror when there was work to be done. She left the publicity to Reggie and he literally had to drag her to functions sometimes. He didn't think she owned formal wear he hadn't paid for.

Which is not to say that she failed to recognize that the publicity from this incident was not every bit as dangerous as the accident itself. In times of crisis, the hand twitches of her Tourette's syndrome became highly exaggerated, and she ticked three times in rapid succession as she sat down at the desk.

"Thanks for coming over tonight," said Reggie. Gina nodded and waited.

"This is the footage. You ready?"

Another brisk nod, this time accompanied by a deep breath.

Reggie unpaused the recording, and Gina watched silently as the train came chugging out of the tunnel. You got a pretty good view of the jump scare from this angle. Eventually, Reggie hoped to install a camera in the shark's mouth in order to record HD reaction shots and videos to sell or use for promotion.

Probably a good thing he hadn't gotten around to that.

There was Micah, small and vulnerable in the screen, excitedly pointing at the pool. He was leaning some, but he was still seated perfectly firm on the train like a good boy should.

Then the shark rose from the water and snatched him away. Reggie was glad there was no audio.

Gina watched the whole incident, all the way to the point where Reggie, Keesha, and Aaron drove off, without comment. Then she took the remote from Reggie and began playing it back and forth, stopping at different points to look at things. Reggie let her work, knowing better than to interrupt her. He took this moment to go to the bathroom and then grab a soda from the mini fridge. When he came back, she was massaging the bridge of her nose with her left hand while she jotted stuff down on a notepad.

"Sorry," she said. "I've got a pressure headache from the flight. Got a Coke for me?"

Reggie did.

"This shouldn't have happened," she said, turning to the video. "This should have been impossible. Look here. See how far the shark jumps? You can actually see the launch machinery at the back. I remember when we installed it. I had you move the train for hours so we could test that at no angle was it possible to see the machine parts from any point on the train at any time. There's more than a yard of it exposed here."

"But the machine can extend that far even if we didn't program it that way, right?" asked Reggie.

"Well, yes," said Gina. "We got the basic kit from an old haunted house set-up, remember? The pneumatic reach is quite a bit longer than you actually use because that way you can install it in more places and have it jump out of deeper hiding spots. It wasn't a shark initially. I think it was some kind of ghost or guy with a chainsaw that came roaring out of a closet and then followed people for a bit. We had that art car guy make the shark bits."

Clearly, it wasn't impossible. Somehow, one way or another, the programming was changed, and the reach of the shark was extended. It was a software problem, not a hardware or guest negligence one.

Removing the shark entirely was a tremendous pain in the ass. The installation was dug into a deep pit that sometimes required oxygen masks to go down and work on it if the drainage system was clogged with leaves. It was a nasty business even when all you were doing was checking the lubricants, to say nothing of getting the whole rotten bastard out of there. In fact, Reggie was pretty sure that they hadn't even left some sort of access to the furthermost bolts. They might have to bring in a digger just to get to them or use a crane to rip it out completely.

"So what's the plan?" asked Reggie. "You want to try and take it apart, remove it, what?"

"Taking it apart and moving it would effectively shut down the park for at least four days," said Gina. "There are too many cross-patched electrical systems that run through the grid there. We'll have to run the tanks on emergency power and can't risk the rides or even the internal lights. People might bump into things and hurt themselves.

"And that's just getting it out. What do you want me to do with it once I've got it out? I can check all the systems from fore to aft, maybe shorten the reach if you want to spend about $5,000. Then we have to put it all back. That, at least, would be faster, but we're looking at a week's closure."

Reggie got up and walked away from the desk. From his window, he could see down into the ghost-lit park. The flamingoes quietly waded in their lake by the picnic area, and in the distance, the fake torches illuminated the entrance to the shark tunnel. All was very silent.

The most moral thing would be to remove the attraction entirely, of course. On the other hand, it was just a machine, no different from the train that ran by it. A darker, more cynical part of him was aware that the legend of the mechanical shark would probably do more good than harm to his attendance once it took hold, and he had to consider that. After all, Micah wasn't going to die from a broken arm. Probably wouldn't even suffer any real impairment.

Maybe, just maybe, they could solve this by looking just at the programming.

Reggie pushed a button on his phone.

"Tovar, here, Mr. Roberts," said his night watchman on his rounds. Normally he'd be in Reggie's office watching the cameras, only occasionally venturing out onto the grounds to check things. After being briefed and hearing about the meeting, he decided to take an early lunch and keep busy poking about until needed.

"Hey Tovar," said Reggie. "Here's what we're going to do. You and I and are going to go down to maintenance and get some of those tarps and freestanding poles that we use when the aquariums are under repair. We're going to block off the shark lagoon until further notice while Gina plays with the programming. I don't want anyone to see it activate or anything while she's working tomorrow."

"*Si*, Mr. Roberts," said Tovar.

"Good man," said Reggie. "See you at maintenance."

The phone barked electronically and then went out.

"You might as well go home, Gina," said Reggie. "We'll re-plug the shark in, and you can start on the software tomorrow. No sense in you messing with it right now while we're reconnecting."

Gina stood and stretched. She nodded and began printing out computer logs to look at when she got home. With a perfunctory goodbye, Reggie left to meet his watchman.

***

It took roughly an hour for the two men to construct the barrier. Tovar was always a whirlwind of efficiency, with never a wasted movement. Reggie was mostly there to hold things that he was instructed to hold and do the final reconnect with his keys. Tovar had even thought to bring freestanding lights to better illuminate them, though it made Reggie feel like they were digging a midnight grave.

The shark regarded them just above the water with indifferent patience.

The poles and blue tarps made an ugly curtain across the pool roughly a foot from the train tracks. Reggie disabled the trip switch while Tovar made up a sign that said "Under Maintenance" to attach to the shroud. Afterward, the two men waded to the back and very hesitantly Reggie reconnected the power settings. Tovar looked into the pool passively. He wasn't easily rattled.

When the final switch was flipped, the shark made a humming sound, and the pneumatics hissed as it slipped silently into the water. Now it was all but invisible. Suddenly, Reggie really didn't want to wade past it but felt silly after watching Tovar do so without any qualm. There wasn't anything to do but follow.

Equipment tucked away and riding back to the office in Tovar's golf cart to change, the night watchman was upbeat and chatty. He recognized the tragedy that had happened today, but his job was often very dull, and this was a welcome distraction from watching cameras and studying for nursing school.

"I hope we can get the shark back on track," he said merrily. "My son loves that thing. Shame about that kid getting hurt, but I'm sure there's an easy solution."

"Hope so," said Reggie. Christ, he was tired, and Tovar's energy made him feel even more tired.

"Gina will figure it out," said Tovar with confidence. He was fond of the gruff engineer and never doubted her. "Probably just a bad update or something, you know?"

"A what?" asked Reggie.

"You know, a system update," said Reggie rambling on. "Happens on my computer all the time. Some mandatory update comes down from the parent company automatically, and you restart the computer, and the next thing you know, half the text is in Portuguese and the F button turns off the sound now. They usually fix it pretty fast in another download. You don't even notice it most of the time. Probably happens a lot less to guys that don't buy their computers off Craigslist."

Tovar laughed, but Reggie wondered if he was right.

***

The next morning, Reggie woke as usual, but was for all intents and purposes, he was little more than a collection of sore muscles and a repository for black coffee. Thankfully, his niece had gotten up for school early and left him breakfast and the pot already filled. Joanna was a good kid who happily kept house for him in exchange for a rent-free place to live within biking distance of the University of St. Thomas. Days like today, where he found a prepared meal waiting on a plate in the oven, he seriously wondered if it might be worth it to pay her way through a doctorate just to enjoy four more years of this. College was expensive, but waking up to fresh bacon was priceless.

As he munched, he pulled up the *Houston Post* news blog on his phone. Yep, there it was on the front page and already making its way like a plague through social media. Thankfully, Keesha had treated him with the utmost professionalism, and Reggie actually admired Aaron's picture of the shark leaping from the blood-tinted water. The shot had caught the shark on a retraction, which made it look like it didn't come as close to the train as the security footage clearly showed. The story framed the incident as a freak accident and kindly mentioned it was the first hospitalization of an attendee at the Houston Maritime Adventure.

Some quick searching showed the other media outlets were just feeding from Keesha's trough. One TV station got a hold of a large woman and her two sons who were willing to express their fear and terror on camera, but neither Craig nor Micah Ochoa's names appeared anywhere. With any luck, this would go away.

Reggie dressed and drove to the park. There were still two hours before opening, plenty of time to touch base and make plans. The first thing he did was walk the track, unlocking the shark tunnel as he did so. Outside the exit, the tarps were undisturbed. He peeked through a gap and saw nothing but the unbroken, placid surface of the water. If he squinted, he could just make out the head of the shark.

In the office, Reggie greeted Tovar, who, as usual, looked like he could run a marathon, even after having probably been up for fourteen hours. He had class today and gave his boss a quick breakdown of the otherwise quiet night so he could beat the traffic into the medical center. With an affectionate pat on the shoulder for the old man, Tovar left, and Reggie got to work.

The main controls for the shark were located in a server room in the backstage areas of the shark tunnel. Reggie dipped and ducked through the maze of pipes and filters that kept the sharks happy and healthy, relieved at last to see the server room door slightly ajar with the light on.

Gina sat cross-legged on the floor, e-cigarette dangling from her neck holder. She was syncing her tablet to the PC, trying to get into the code that determined the shark's movements.

Without looking up, she addressed Reggie.

"Practical stuff first," she said. "I'm draining the pool now so that when I activate the shark the water jets will just suck air and we won't have them blowing down the barrier or making banging noises all the livelong day. That is, so far, the only good news."

"Is there any opposite of good news, or is it just no news?" asked Reggie.

"I honestly haven't looked into this program since we installed the shark," said Gina. "I'm relatively certain this isn't my coding because I'm also relatively certain I'm not completely whack-a-mole. There's no vector assigned for distance on the damned thing. It's some sort of weird algorithm attached to the velocity of the trip switch. Almost like a tennis video game."

"*No te entiendo*," said Reggie. "*Puede hablar Ingles?*"

"Your Spanish is getting better, at least," said Gina with a rare grin. "Basically, the shark is programmed to track the switch on the train. It's not like pulling a lever. How it attacks is actually guided by the sensors in the computer. In essence, it can 'see' you when you drive by, and its leap is calculated a certain way so it comes within a certain distance and chomps for a certain amount of time."

"It's designed to be scary, is that it?" asked Reggie.

"Bingo," replied Gina. "It's a pretty neat thing to do. I'd be slightly impressed, except I can't figure out why it went from 'be scary' to 'be really extra special scary.' I'm going to go through the update logs here in a minute, once this syncs. I'm curious how long this has been going on. If you want to help, you might try going through the security footage over the past couple of months, and see if you notice any difference in the patterns."

"Sounds better than sitting in the sun all day," said Reggie. "I honestly didn't have the heart to play engineer this morning. Meet me for lunch, and we'll see where we are."

Back in the office with a cold soda beside him, Reggie rubbed his neck, and began pulling up the footage. Luckily, the system was designed to capture and compile motion, and since the only time there was any motion in that area was when the train was coming through, it was relatively easy to set some guidelines. Within fifteen minutes, he had about an hour's worth of shots going back approximately three months. He instructed the system to start from the beginning, sat back, and watched.

Two months ago, there was the shark leaping straight out of the water at the train. It clearly came no closer than eight feet from the cars. Same thing about two weeks in, but Reggie rewound the footage and noticed that the leaps were no longer quite as straight. They were angled and seemed to follow individual passengers. It was barely noticeable, but once you realized it, you couldn't miss it.

About a month ago, the footage started getting terrifying. First, the movements of the mouth were no longer redundant. It wasn't opening or closing on a cycle, but with a clear wait until it was at the apex of its leap. Only after that initial slam of metal teeth would the opening and closing commence with regularity.

Second, the shark was most definitely aiming at children. It was hard to tell because most of the people that took the train did so as families, but whenever an adult was sitting on the side with the shark, it would ignore them in favor of a seat where a child was seated closer to it.

Which was all academic, maybe even desirable from an entertainment standpoint, but as he watched the last week leading up

58

to the attack, he saw the evidence with his own eyes. The shark's range doubled and then tripled until finally it had just the right amount of reach to grab someone.

What in the hell was going on?

His phone squawked. "Reggie?"

"Yeah, Gina?" he responded.

"I'm done down here and getting ready to head up to you," she said. "Pick us up some burgers from the stands on my way up?"

"That would be nice," he said. "Thanks. See you in a minute."

***

They ate in silence. Reggie didn't have much of an appetite, and neither did Gina. They ate mindlessly because they knew they were probably going to need the energy, not because they were hungry. Reggie did his best not to think about what he'd seen yesterday. He wished Gina had suggested salads instead.

Full, they threw away what was left, and Gina began.

"This is bad, boss," she said, looking over the tops of her glasses. Her tics, absent when engrossed in her work but now back, were so fierce they interrupted her speech slightly. No wonder she'd suggested food that didn't require a fork.

"I'm not going to sugarcoat this; we have a monster," she said. "A literal, not at all figurative, monster, like the one Frankenstein built. It has to be removed.

"The original set up came from a company called Bottlerocket out of Lebanon, Indiana. Just a couple of dudes building robots for fun and selling them out as attractions. They did everything from haunted houses to Freddy Fazbear's Pizza. Only they closed around 2006 when one of the guys was in a car accident.

"They sold their assets, including customer information and programming contracts, to another company called Kaneko. Kaneko did a little of everything. Standalone handheld games, little toy dogs that bark and they also provided service for animatronics. Repairing them and updating them so their code could be integrated into more modern systems. Kaneko is who we worked with when we refurbished the shark.

"Except Kaneko is gone now, too. They went bankrupt in 2012. They were sold piecemeal, and here's why we're in trouble. Over a dozen companies picked up pieces of the pie, and even then, a few of them have been dissolved, merged, or whatever. Somewhere in that corporate mishmash, there is a server quietly updating our shark, and God alone knows what else out there in the world, and it's turning it into something that scares the crap out of me."

"So you're saying someone is hacking animatronics?" Reggie asked.

"No, that's dumb," said Gina. "I mean, it's probably not that. I don't think there's some psychopathic programmer out there tweaking our database and laughing like a Bond villain. I don't think they even know what it's doing, and I'm willing to bet it's not even a person at all.

"What I think, is that somewhere in all of those database transfers, our shark, which is hardwired into the same system we use to do payroll, run the lights, feed the tanks, and everything, got

60

piggybacked into something else. Could be anything. Could be someone is out there making an AI for a video game shark, or maybe someone is writing a program for security cameras, or maybe it's an automatic auction app, and the shark computer is translating it as best it can.

"Point is, we'll never find it. There's too much to trace through, and even if I tear out the whole code and do my own, I have zero guarantees that some 3 a.m. update won't just rewrite over it.

"My advice is cut the power and pour concrete over the thing. I'm not joking in the slightest. That footage is all the proof we need. There is no telling what else will start getting rewritten, now that some sort of programming fuck-uppery has found its way into the system. Salt. The. Earth."

***

After Gina left the office, Reggie sat and thought about what she had said. For all her work with the cold hard world of machines and code, she did have something of a reputation as a bit of a weirdo. Reggie knew she kept sage in her desk, had an old pirate coin as a good luck charm, and refused to drink water from the tap. It was not outside the realm of possibility that she honestly thought the shark was somehow haunted.

There wasn't any arguing with her analysis of the code problems, though. He was more worried about some sort of ride breakdown or damage to the heaters that maintained the water temperatures for the fish than anything else. Something had gotten in through the shark, and was eating its way into dangerous territory.

On the screen above him, Reggie looked at the ugly blue tarp barrier that covered the beast. The image was static, taking a shot every ten seconds it didn't detect movement to save space in the databa…

No, it was recording in real time. What the hell?

There was nothing to be seen, but for some reason, the camera seemed to think there was. Reggie pulled out his reading glasses and squinted. He could just make out an edge of the tarp near the tunnel exit that had come loose. It was flapping gently in the wind like a flag.

And here I was, calling Gina paranoid, he thought.

It was only 2 p.m. now, but Reggie was running on fumes after being up late the previous night. He decided to take a brief nap on the couch in the side office. When he woke up and was in a little less jumpy mood, he'd get a couple of staffers to come with him and remove the power couplings permanently from the shark and then cut every cable they could find. Gina could confirm they'd eliminated access, and then yes, he'd fill in the pool with cement. A rowboat with a bite hole and an old skeleton would do just fine to replace it. The head could rust underground for all he cared.

As he walked into the adjacent doorway toward his nap the flapping tarp settled down, and the footage played in real-time for a few seconds longer before returning to ten-second stills. Soon, the only movement around was the gentle air current of Reggie's snores.

***

He woke with a start from a dream about lions in the jungle. Their roars were ringing in his ears when he realized that it was actually the sound of a heavy rain outside. Groggy, he took out his phone and saw that it was after 8 p.m. The park was closed, and since he'd asked the staff not to disturb him, he'd gone ahead and slept through it. Christ, he should get up and check that everything had been settled correctly. He wondered if there was anyone left to go help him with the shark. Tovar wouldn't be in tonight, and the other watchman, Mike, was generally useless for anything except his specific task of watching the screens.

First things first, he thought. Reggie got up to go to the bathroom, wash his face, and make some attempt at smoothing his shirt. He wished for coffee, but settled for chugging a Coke instead for the caffeine.

Back in his office chair, he rang down to the main office. Sinead, his afternoon manager, said she was just about to lock the door and drive off. She hadn't even realized that Reggie was still there. She gave him a brief breakdown of the day. No incidents to report, money in the deposit box, everything hunk-dory. No, she'd already seen all the staff clock out, sorry. Did he need her help?

Reggie briefly considered it, but Sinead had two young children in school who would only get a brief story with their mama as it was tonight, assuming she didn't miss bedtime completely in this weather. It was just a machine, he thought, unplug it and stop being a baby.

"No, hun," he said. "Leave the lights on a bit longer. I've got a quick thing to do. See you tomorrow."

Cursing to himself, Reggie grabbed rain gear out of the closet. He hated the big, flappy yellow things. They always retained the smell of the polluted air the rain fell through, and whenever he looked in the mirror while wearing one, he felt like a racist caricature, though he couldn't really put his finger on why. Something about it screamed "Old funny black dude in a horror film about to get murdered" to him.

I need to quit thinking and get the hell out of here, he thought. Come on, man. Just one little thing and then you can have dinner, a bath, a drink, maybe take the day off tomorrow. See a movie, hit a museum, maybe just stay in and read a book.

As he made his way through the park, Reggie kept on listing all the wonderful things he would do tomorrow that did not involve being here. He decided to cut through the shark tunnel to make sure Gina wasn't still hanging out in the server room. Plus, it would give him a chance to get out of the rain.

How do you feel about Skee ball, Reggie? I feel just fine about Skee ball, and I don't give a toss if a grown man shouldn't be in Chuck E. Cheese playing it by himself. Maybe Joanna and I could have lunch. I could catch up with *Game of Thrones*…

The looming doors of the Maison Rouge, lit by fake torchlight, rose up in front of him, but yielded easily to his master key. Through the pirate hideout, he walked the tracks, glad to be out of the rain. He pushed back his hood and left a trail of rainwater behind him. He patted Jean Lafitte on the knee as he went through the door.

The hurricane effects were activated by the train, which meant it was quiet but dark. Reggie walked carefully on the downgrade, making sure not to trip on the crossties or slip in his wet shoes. The bottom of the tunnel was completely black as the rain clouds covered up the moonlight from above. Reggie turned on his flashlight and watched one of the large bull sharks dart away from the sudden illumination.

People rarely came down to the tunnel at night, and all around him the sharks seemed to regard him as an intruder. During the day, they swam with languid apathy, only ever showing energy when feeding time came. Now, they thrashed and came close to the glass. The sand tiger glided over his head like some sort of fanged, pale cloud.

Make cookies. Fire up the grill. Maybe go down to the gun range. Reggie kept listing like it was a prayer as he scuttled down the tunnel feeling like bait. Off to the side,

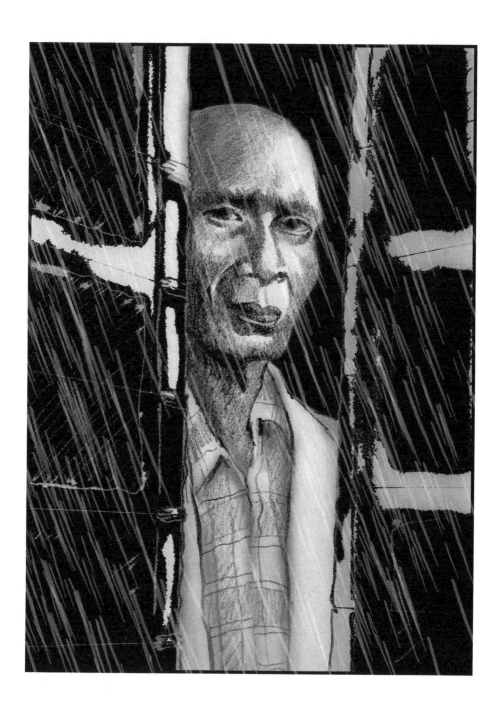

he spied the door to the back area. He opened it and noticed all the lights were off here too. He turned them on, made his way to the back, but Gina was nowhere to be found.

OK, he thought, just me then.

Back in the tunnel, he climbed the ramp to the exit doors. With a deep breath, he unlocked them. The rain was still intense, and he quickly put his hood back up. The wind had blown several of the poles down from Tovar's and his makeshift barrier. The shark was partially covered by the tarps. The rain had refilled the pool slightly, but it still was only a few inches deep. Not deep enough to hide the ugly mechanical aspects that snaked into the rock wall behind it. It gave Reggie the weird feeling of walking in on a surgical procedure.

At least he wouldn't have to wade this time. Reggie hugged the edge of the building, trying hard to stay out of the water completely as well as not slip. He was no longer even pretending he wasn't freaked out, and he couldn't decide if he wished he could see the shark's head or not.

Bookstore. I'll go spend an hour at the bookstore picking out something new, and then get a bottle of something nice from the liquor store across the street. Yes, no matter what, I think a trip to the liquor store is in order, don't you Reggie? Yes, sir, I do.

The water jets went off like gun shots.

There wasn't enough liquid in the pool to spray much, and no one could possibly be any wetter in this downpour anyway, but the sound spooked Reggie so badly that he slipped and fell hard into the deep puddle. The impact knocked the wind out of him and he was relatively certain a little bit of urine, too. Double vision slowly came and went, just in time for him to see something out of a nightmare.

The shark rose, not fast, but with majestic slowness to the absolute end of its hydraulic reach as the tarp and poles fell off it. Fourteen, eighteen, maybe twenty feet in the air. From where Reggie lay at its base, it was like seeing a skyscraper come to life. Machinery hissed, and suddenly, the head came crashing down with force enough to shatter masonry. The eyes never moved, they couldn't move, but something in the shark sensed Reggie was there.

Reggie scrambled to his feet, desperate to make it around the building and to the power switch, but another blast from the water jets caught him right in the face. This time he stumbled backward but managed to keep his wits and feet. He wiped his eyes clear just in time to recoil and duck under the sudden attack from the shark head. Its metal teeth clanged so hard they gave off sparks, and the rain steamed from the friction heat. As fast as he could, Reggie scrambled backwards, hoping to get out of the shark's range.

Hanging onto the door of the tunnel, he watched something terrible unfold. The shark lunged and brought its mouth down on the train tracks. Nothing happened for a moment, and then a horrendous screeching noise began to pierce the thunder. Unbelievably, the shark was tearing itself away from its mountings, the bolts groaning and the cables snapping like severed intestines. With single-minded determination, the head yanked and pulled.

It'll cut its own power, thought Reggie. I don't know why the hell it's doing this, but if it breaks free, problem solved.

Call your brother tomorrow. We could play cards. Maybe dominoes. Please, God, I just want to play dominoes. That's not too much to ask, is it?

The shriek of tearing metal was deafening, and with a final, mighty pull the shark dragged its mechanical support system free, and then lay still. It rolled to its side on the slick rocks, hindquarters sparking here and there. The sparks seemed very bright until Reggie realized that all the lights in the park had gone out when the shark severed its link. With a throbbing hum, he heard the backup generators that kept the heat and filtration systems going start up.

The shark didn't move, and Reggie was certain that it was powerless now that it was disconnected. Not quite certain enough to walk past it, though. Instead, he would go back the way he came. Never turning around, he re-entered the tunnel and locked the doors behind him.

If he thought it was dark in the shark tunnel before, it was nothing compared to now. For one thing, he'd dropped his flashlight sometime during the attack. Frightened, he took out his phone, thankful he'd put it on the charger before lying down. He flicked on an app that activated the camera flash as a makeshift flashlight. It was murder on the battery and nowhere as good as a proper light, but it was better than nothing.

The sharks were truly agitated now, probably sensing a difference in their usual, endless routine. One of the bulls actually bumped hard into the glass as Reggie passed, which almost made him drop his phone. He didn't think the sharks could break through the thick barrier, but a lot of things he never thought would happen were going on tonight.

With as much dignity and grace as he could muster, Reggie retraced his steps through the tunnel. He briefly thought of going into the server room to check things, but at this point he honestly didn't care what happened as long as he got out of here.

He was barely twenty feet down the hall when the banging started.

Reggie stopped in his tracks, knees shaking. He looked back over his shoulder, hoping against hope what he was hearing was the sound of sharks fighting amongst themselves or the roof above being ripped off by the wind. Literally anything but the animatronic beating at the locked door.

There was a crash, a GASHUNK, and around the curve and down the grade it came, jaws opening and closing and front fins flapping. Behind where the dorsal fin would be on a live shark was something resembling a rotting, un-cared for car piston. The shark moved like an inchworm, diving forward and then dragging its metal end behind it. With the full range of its hydraulic press being used, it was covering ground much faster than Reggie could believe. Silent save for the groan of metal on stone, it was coming for him.

How does it still have power? he thought.

Reggie ran, taking the curve badly and sliding on wet shoes hard enough to crash into the side of the tunnel. Sharks swarmed to where he was, snapping ineffectually at the glass. Seconds later he heard the sound of the massive robot ramming into the side of the tunnel behind him where he had just been… then an even more sickening noise.

The live sharks in the tanks couldn't break the glass, but the robot could.

If his stalker hadn't been so silent he would never have been able to mark the sound of glass beginning to crack and water beginning to slowly gush into the tunnel. There was no time for Reggie to look back and see what was going on, but he imagined a tidal wave surging over him - full to the brim with hungry, extremely agitated sharks. Would the savage bulls get him first, or would they allow their new metal king his prize? He didn't think he'd be lucky enough to drown.

Run, old man. Run!

He met the hill up and out of the tunnel, walking almost on all fours to grasp crossties and keep from slipping. As he gained the top of the ramp, he spared the briefest of glances back. In the dim light that filtered in from the open door of the Maison Rouge, Reggie could see the water level was rising, but there was no sign of the shark. Maybe the slick upgrade would be too much for it.

It burst from the black water, teeth seizing on the ground at the top of the hill. It struggled to bring up its heavy back end, dead eyes never leaving Reggie's face. Try as it might, it seemed like a simple incline was going to defeat this abomination.

Reggie kept backing away as it retractedt, slipped, and redoubled its efforts to come after him. The structure all around him protested the monster that had been let loose inside it. It had been built to withstand a hurricane, but never this. Diving out the door, Reggie watched as the building seemed to explode. The roof drove down on top of the tank it was housing, and water gushed from every possible exit like someone had squeezed a Twinkie in the middle.

An unfamiliar noise started to fill the sudden silence after the collapse. It was an odd thumping, and Reggie realized it was the big sharks thrown free in the collapse and now flopping desperately toward any water they could find. In the dark, he almost missed four hundred pounds of a dying, but still deadly, bull shark as it bucked powerfully past his head.

With the final impossibility that he was now dodging regular flesh and blood sharks on land, the last of Reggie's bravery left him, and he tore off into the rain as fast as his legs could carry him.

***

He woke to the sound of his phone playing the theme from *Jaws*. For a moment, he couldn't remember where he was, and then it all came back to him. He'd driven to the Westin Galleria Hotel and insisted on a room as high in the sky as they could give him. Once he was a couple hundred feet above sea level, he'd ordered a bottle of vodka, and it took more than half of it to get him to sleep. Even then, he'd dreamed of being caught in a shipwreck, pursued by a Kraken that squeezed its way through impossibly small doors after him.

His phone kept ringing, and reluctantly he answered it. The *Jaws* theme was his ringtone for his staff members. Just a little joke.

It was Gina. Of course it was.

"Yes?" he answered. "What! No, you've got to be kidding me! The whole tunnel collapsed? No, I left shortly after close last night and went home sick. Look, I'll be right there. Just hang on."

Reggie hung up, unhappy to have lied to Gina but not willing to admit what happened. He dressed, went down to the mall and bought a fresh set of clothes, and then drove to work after changing. His hands shook so hard, he could barely start the car.

In the daylight, the damage to his beloved park was even worse. The smell of rotting fish was everywhere. Keesha was leaning by the gate opposite of Gina, each eyeing the other with detached distrust. Normally, Reggie would be worried about the press, but not today. Today nothing Keesha could ever put in print was worse than what he'd been through.

"Reggie!" the two women said, almost together.

"Hi, Gina," he replied. "Hello, Keesha. Suppose we might as well just get all the unpleasant explanations and discoveries out of the way at once. Lead on, Gina."

They picked their way through the park, avoiding the deeper puddles. Rather than follow the tracks, Gina led them directly through the trees, several of which had blown over in the wind. Ahead, where the expansive building holding predators from the seven seas once proudly stood, was simply nothing. Coming out of the trees, Reggie groaned.

There was a small lake, with the crushed, crumpled roof of the old shark tunnel sticking up in twisted spires. Within the brackish water, dorsal fins swirled and swarmed. There was enough frozen bait housed in there to feed them for maybe a week, and then they would turn on each other if they weren't recovered. The railroad tracks rose out of the water, and there was no sign of where the mechanical shark had once frightened and delighted people.

Not far away, Reggie stared at the fat corpse of the bull shark that had almost gotten him on its way to asphyxiation. It was still, but that no longer suited Reggie as an indicator of safe.

"There is no good news," said Gina, and Keesha began writing down. "The tunnel is a total loss, and that means the park is a near-total loss. Half the HQ was down there, and it's all wrecked. The main aquarium is still running on backup generators, and we might be able to get them grid power soon, but all the rides and other stuff ran through that hub. It'll take months to fix, and that's only if the city shells out the big bucks. Considering, that as far as anyone can tell right now, the building just collapsed on its own, I doubt they're going to be very optimistic about it."

Reggie did his best to look sad, but honestly, he couldn't care less. He was searching the waterline very carefully.

"Here's the really bad news," said Gina, and she turned to Keesha. "Write this down verbatim because it is very important. Several of the sharks were washed out into Buffalo Bayou. Most of them will be dead by tomorrow. They can't handle the freshwater, but we can only account for one of the bulls. That means a huge hungry shark is either dead at the bottom of the tunnel or swimming around in the bayou in a very bad mood."

Keesha wrote furiously. Reggie realized that the city was never going to recoup this. Not with him at the head, anyway. Not after he'd dropped a monster into a body of water that ran through the whole of Houston.

"I've contacted the people we acquire sharks from, and they're getting ready to send a team down here to start looking for the shark. Until then, people need to stay the hell away from the water."

Great, thought Reggie. Just great.

"I lied. There is one bit of good news," said Gina. "Something even worse could have been let loose last night." Reggie looked at her in terror. She gave him a glance and then led Keesha and him away.

Around the edge of the lake, they slogged through wet ground. Eventually, they made their way to drier stuff, and Reggie realized he was on the embankment that overlooked where Boris was kept.

The solid concrete wall now featured a huge, gaping hole. The entire wall had collapsed, and the water that streamed into the saltwater crocodile's enclosure now formed a waterfall into the bayou. It was like looking at a scene after an apocalypse.

Gina tapped him on the shoulder, and he looked where she indicated. There was Boris. The huge croc had been bitten nearly in half. Reggie climbed the maintenance ladder down, followed by the two women.

"We figure the bull did that," said Gina. "My guess is the water initially washed her this way, and her and Boris got crossways. Either some wreckage smashed against the wall with enough force to tear a hole or all the water just caused a structural weakness and it collapsed. Either way, that's where the shark made it into the water, but at least it wasn't a giant crocodile, right?"

Reggie agreed absentmindedly as Keesha took shots. Poor Boris. It looked as if he'd rushed at something, only to end up in a set of jaws past his front legs. One bite later, and the mightiest living reptile was a hunk of dead meat.

Down on the ground, something glimmered dully. Reggie reached down to pick it up. It was a shark's tooth, covered in blood.

A metal one.

He told himself that it was possible the tooth had simply washed here, and Gina's speculation was correct. He reminded himself that the shark was just a machine running off a power line and didn't dare face the fact that even after tearing free of that line it had come for him. Even a saltwater croc had clearly been no match.

Through the hole in the cement, Reggie stared out into the Buffalo Bayou. Later today or early tomorrow, Keesha would correctly report there was something dangerous in the waterways of Houston. Reggie remembered reading about the drowned catacombs downtown after Tropical Storm Allison and all the myriad of places underground that were only a concrete wall away from the bayou.

Part of him also thought of how many of those lost, forgotten animatronics were hanging around in the world, quietly being updated by a system that didn't even know it had gone mad. What was waking up out there?

76

Please, God, thought Reggie, let it only be a shark in the water. Just a shark.

Nevaeh

NAME.

Lissa started to write "Lissa Niermann," changed her mind halfway through and made an ugly grey space erasing on the form, in which she wrote "Alice Niermann". Employment applications were official... right? They got sent to the government, and they couldn't keep track of your taxes if you didn't give them your full name, right? Lissa didn't want to go to jail for tax evasion just because she hated being called Alice.

Maybe it wouldn't matter now, anyway. Maybe Woodlake's would take one look at the smudgy mess she'd already made and decide she was too stupid to even write her name on the first try, let alone serve customers their prayers.

Lissa sighed and finished the form, sitting on the hard, white plastic booth, trying hard to concentrate. The upbeat Christian pop music played slightly too loud, and the children were roughhousing in the jungle gym. Still not convinced that she had not inadvertently committed a federal crime during the process, she walked over to the counter and handed the paper in with as perky a smile as she could muster.

"Thank you... Alice," said the manager, briefly glancing at her application. He was the single largest man that Lissa had ever seen in person, easily three times her own diminutive mass.

"You're welcome," she replied, all pep and hope that she was certain did not mask her desperation to be employed. "When do you think I might hear back about a job?"

"Oh, I'll put this right on top of the box, little lady," he said with a strangely high giggle to his voice. The small laugh reminded her of a pebble dropped in a pond as it seemed to roll down from his mouth through the folds of his flesh. "I know we need people, especially for the night shift, so we'll start calling people early next week, I think. I'll keep you in mind."

"Thanks so much," said Lissa. "I check my messages between classes, so if I don't answer, you can leave a message."

"Will do," said the manager. "Go on, now, and let me get back to work. You have a blessed day, you hear?'

"I hear," she said and walked outside.

The second the pop music and murmur of customers were cut off by the door, Lissa suddenly felt very tired. It had been a long day at school, and there was still homework and chores waiting for her at the other end of the two-mile walk home. Her backpack cut deep lashes into her shoulders, deep enough the skin was often red and irritated when she undressed to bathe at the end of the night. It reminded her of *The Scarlet Letter* she'd read in class last year. The priest (or was it a reverend?) had been into whipping himself over the shoulder for impure thoughts. There was a word for that, but she couldn't recall it. She remembered she thought to take off all your clothes and whip yourself was dirtier than any thought she'd ever had about another person.

"Self-flegation? No, I don't think that's a real word," she muttered to herself as she began to trudge home.

It was fall, and the days were already getting darker, even if the weather was not actually all that colder. The sun had gone down just enough for Woodlake's outside lights to come on, beckoning those in need of salvation and spiritual guidance from out of the dark. A line of cars snaked around in the drive-thru. Proudly, the signed proclaimed, "ONE MILLION SAVED... AND COUNTING!"

***

It was full dark at home, and her mom was not overly happy about that.

"You know I don't like it when you come home late," said her mom. Ms. Liu was so severe, she was almost a caricature, which usually happened when you based your entire life philosophy on books you bought in the grocery store.

"I'm not really late," said Lissa, and eased off her backpack. "It just gets dark earlier now, is all. Besides, I had to fill out an application at Woodlake's, remember? They're hiring."

"Yes, yes, I remember," said her mom. "But you still need to be home on time so you can make sure you get your homework done early enough for me to check it."

Ms. Liu walked away from Lissa in mid-sentence, pulling out the chair to the dining room table with its impressively bright study lamp as she went past. Lissa didn't sigh, didn't yell, didn't follow her mother to continue to try and establish the absolute veracity of who was right and who was in error in this particular disagreement, and she most certainly did not cry.

Her mom loved her, she was sure, but her mom loved the idea of her being the perfectly bright and obedient child more. Ms. Liu was only half-Chinese and looked almost completely Caucasian, while Lissa, at one-fourth, looked like she just stepped off a boat. At least, until she opened her mouth and the Texas twang came out. Lissa was certain that a part of her mom resented this, and that resentment tended to manifest as pathological attachments to American pseudo-Chinese philosophies like Tiger Mother parenting.

So for the next half hour, Lissa did her calculus, and then for another she sat pretending to do her calculus until her mother came over to check her work while Lissa made dinner. Her work was perfect in both regards, an achievement marked only by a lack of pointing out that it was not perfect.

Ms. Liu talked about her employees at the bank. Lissa talked about school and thought about the car she would buy if she got her job.

***

A week later, on another grey Tuesday afternoon, Lissa sat in the cramped manager's office watching a series of videos that were supposed to introduce her to the wonderful world of working at

Woodlake's, your primary source for salvation on the go. The brown-haired man in the suit seemed like he was directly talking to her on the other side of the high-definition television. His movements felt impossibly sharp.

"Woodlake's grew out of a movement to try and bring the full backing and power of the massive Woodlake Church facility in Houston to small-town America in a way that was more personal than merely watching our ratings-shattering services on the television. We wanted the faithful to be able to interact one on one, face to face, with specifically trained deliverers of the Lord's message in order to help them through their trials and tribulations. Affordable and on-the-go ministering is the aim of every Woodlake's franchise."

Under a strange, toneless jazzy version of a hymn, Lissa watched wave after wave of clean-cut deacons in their spotless red uniforms reach through the drive-thru windows to clasp hands with a line of troubled folks. They recited the company approved prayers with huge smiles and loud, happy voices, often bringing tears to the eyes of all involved.

Once the prayer was finished up, the customers would make a donation ("By cash or credit card, and which, in the great spirit of America, is fully tax-deductible," said the man), or perhaps purchase some of the items that were part of the "menu" offered by the store.

Mission, the manager had told her. Woodlake's was a mission, not a store.

The bumper stickers were popular. Especially the pro-life ones as well as the ones that declared the driver was for guns, god, and... well, the third word seemed to change a lot and matter little. You could also buy several of the celebrity pastors' books, often in small kid comic form, as well as pins and buttons, and religious play sets. The available options were numerous enough to offer at least three or four choices in each category, but not numerous enough to overwhelm. Lissa was sure she'd have them all memorized pretty quickly.

Though the drive-thru was the busiest area of the store ("Mission!" thought Lissa), there was a pretty sizable pray-in area that allowed people and families to come in, sit around in a booth, and have a deacon pray with them. People were also allowed to bring meals in with them so that they could have family dinners blessed after they were reheated in the row of microwaves near the back next to a pair of soft drink machines. Beyond that was an enclosed playground with a ball pit, slides, and a tube maze. Another big television in the area showed *VeggieTales* cartoons.

As the last of the training videos finished up, the brown-haired man returned.

"It's because of people like you that Woodlake's has become the number one church in America. Some people sneer and call it Fast Faith, but in a world where everything is so hectic, maybe faith does need to be fast just to catch up."

The music rose to one last limp sting. The screen faded to black with a Bible quote.

84

"God is not unjust; he will not forget your work and the love you have shown him as you have helped his people and continue to help them." -1 John 4:1

Now the room was dark and silent, and Lissa wasn't sure what do to. The manager on duty, who introduced himself as Alonso, had told her that he would come and get her to start her shift. Would he know the video was over? Should she go open the door?

Outside she could hear the low murmur of Woodlake's at one of the slow moments before the main evening rush. Lissa began to think.

Woodlake's wasn't her first choice of after school or weekend employment. She'd wanted to go work at maybe the Brookshire Brothers down the street from school, or perhaps in one of the little boutiques in the Walmart. Neither one was hiring, mostly because neither was particularly thriving. The men and women who worked there were all a decade or more older than Lissa herself. They'd been like her, once, but they'd gotten stuck.

So Woodlake's it was, and it certainly paid alright. Lissa hadn't been much of a regular churchgoer since her mom and dad split up, but she still wore the little silver cross Dad had given her when she turned eleven around her neck. She thought of herself as a Christian in the way she thought of herself as a Texan and an American. It was just something she kind of… was. Not something she actually did.

In fact, in many ways Lissa liked Woodlake's better than the Baptist church that her family went to on occasion. Lissa wasn't under any illusion that the wood paneling that accented the walls had ever actually been a tree, or that the semi-animated, glowing picture of Jesus healing the sick that dominated the main room counted as anything like fine art. Still, she liked it. It was new and fun and clean. Her church always seemed to be needing paint, and it often smelled like mildew after a hard rain.

I can do this, she thought to herself. People needed to feel spiritual. They needed to feel close to Jesus just as badly as they needed to eat or go to the bathroom (The boys' bathroom at Woodlake's was marked with a lion, the girls' with a lamb.) As far as Lissa was concerned, it was a job, and she might really get to help people in the process. The more she considered it, the more she was glad she had accepted.

Eleven dollars an hour, too. She started mentally calculating how long it would take her to get the two-thousand dollars Dexter Lilley's dad wanted for that blue VW Beetle she'd asked him about a couple of weeks ago. Numbers rambled in her head until she was surprised by the office light coming on suddenly when Alonso returned.

"Oh," he said. "Sorry. I forgot to tell you that the lights in here and the bathroom are motion sensitive to conserve electricity. Didn't mean to scare you."

"It's okay," said Lissa. "I finished the videos. When do I start?"

"We've got an hour or so before it gets busy," replied Alonso, looking down at Lissa's black slacks and sneakers. "Your pants are good, but you need to wear a belt next time, and get some black shoes when you can. Sneakers are still okay, but they want them to be all or nearly black. You can also wear a black skirt if you want, but it has to reach past your knee, and you need dress shoes if you do that. Let's get you a top out of the supply closet. You're small or extra small?"

"Usually extra small," said Lissa.

"Well, you might have to use a small if we don't have any extra smalls," said Alonso. "I'll order a couple in any case. Never know when you might lose your shirt."

The older man stared at Lissa in silence for a moment. She realized that he was focused intently at her chest, and wondered if he was thinking about how... small she was. Or about her losing her shirt. It was making her a little uncomfortable.

"That necklace is okay," broke in Alonso. "Management doesn't like girls to wear earrings, but they're a little more lax on necklaces if they're Christian. Just tuck it into your shirt if you're cleaning or something so you don't lose it. Oh, and watch out for the kids with grabby hands. If they see you not paying attention while you're praying with a family or something, they might snatch at it. You know how kids are."

He laughed and Lissa joined in, even though she really didn't know how kids are. She supposed she would find out. Alonso beckoned her out of the office and they went to find her a top. Within an hour she was serving customers, her hair still just slightly damp from the perfunctory baptism as a deacon.

It was, again, after dark when Lissa got home, but her mother seeing her in her uniform no longer made any fuss about it. Homework was English. They were reading *Watership Down*, and Ms. Liu deigned to heat up last night's leftovers. Lissa read at the table about a group of rabbits getting lost in the mist trying to find a new home.

After dinner and in her pajamas, Lissa signed onto her computer in her room to Skype with her dad. Her parents had split up three years ago, but it was only two years ago that Lissa and her mom had moved to Madisonville. The Capital Bank here also served as the regional office hub for fourteen other banks in Texas and Arkansas, so while Ms. Liu was nominally only a branch manager by title, she was paid nearly twice the salary of regular branch managers.

It was a good opportunity, she told Lissa again and again when they left San Marcos, but the move also took her several hours away from her dad. He was a coordinator at the big Job Corps training center there and a rising star in the ranks of the Department of Labor. There was nothing for him but Lissa in the boonies of northeastern Texas, and they had to content themselves with only spending summers together and regular Skypes during the week. She was looking forward to seeing him again in late May, and she would be within driving distance of him when she began attending the University of Texas next fall.

Once the link was established, there was her dad, short and stocky with bushy, sandy-colored hair. He was still in his white shirt and tie. Her dad never hesitated to roll up his sleeves to tackle a physical task, but he considered it blasphemy to loosen his tie before bed. When Lissa was little, she would always try to steal his tie right from around his neck. She still kept a light blue one in her top drawer.

"Hey there, Pie," said her dad with a big smile. "How was your first day at work?"

Lissa always liked talking with her dad. He was the easy-going one in the family, the one who went along to get along and never really demanded much of his girls. It was a pretty big shock to Roger Niermann when his wife insisted that they split up, but he also hadn't fought that hard to keep them all together either. When he said he wanted you to have what made you happy, he always meant that one hundred percent and made up his own happiness however he could in what was left.

"It's kind of a weird job, Dad," said Lissa. "I like it, though. There was this family that came through today. Their little boy's dog had been hit by a car, and they asked me to pray for him to get better. It was… it was really sad, but it seemed like it made him a little happier when I did it."

"I'm sure it did," said her dad. "Did you tell him about Rooster?" Rooster was their Beagle when Lissa was younger. He'd been hit by a car, recovered perfectly, and died fat and happy four years ago on a family trip to the river.

"No," replied Lissa. "We're not really supposed to talk about ourselves. There's like, an official list of prayers that we're supposed to do so that each location gives, you know, the same service. That way people can know what to expect."

"Makes sense," said her dad. "I mean, that's what people need God for, right? The unexpected? You pray when something goes wrong because you're unprepared and need strength, but you also pray when things are going right because no one expects that to last forever. I bet it's nice for folks to know that they're going to have that stability. Reliable service, that's always a good bet."

Lissa and her dad talked for another fifteen minutes or so, mostly about Woodlake's because there weren't any in San Marcos yet. Lissa didn't tell him about the woman who had asked for another deacon after seeing Lissa's face because she was currently pretending it was because the woman could see she was nervous and new, not because she was Asian. She also left out the part about Mr. King from down the street who corrected her Humble Living prayer in an increasingly testy manner and paid for it with a single, crumpled dollar bill.

Her dad asked her if she could marry people now, and she joked that she wasn't even dating anyone. They were laughing when Lissa's mom gave a short knock and walked into the room.

"Time for bed, Alice," she said, coming into the camera's view. "Hello, Roger. Good day?"

"Pretty good, Virginia," replied her dad with his easy smile. "Performance reviews this week. We'll see if they move me up the ladder or if they'll finally figure out I'm winging this gig. You?"

"Some idiot tried to rob the Texarkana branch with an old Nintendo zapper spray painted black," said Lissa's mom with a grin. "The security guard on duty was a big retro game collector and recognized it immediately. Tackled the guy screaming 'DUCK HUNT!' at the top of his lungs."

Lissa watched her parents laugh and wondered why her mom hadn't told her the funny story over dinner earlier. Adults were weird. Half an hour later, she was lying on her back in the dark room practicing her prayers and wondered if this counted as "saying" your prayers. She fell asleep in the middle of something about going down to the water.

***

It was Wednesday, and Lissa was walking home from school beside Dexter. She didn't really have a lot of friends, though there wasn't anyone she could think of that out-and-out disliked her. Her habit of reading quietly to herself during lunch and her mom's rather stringent curfew kept her from forming any really deep bonds. She wasn't an artist or an athlete with a passion, and she had no real extracurricular activities outside of yearbook.

Dexter lived three houses down from her, and because he hated riding the noisy school bus with the ripped seats as much as she did, the two had sort of fallen into the habit of keeping each other company to and from school. He was Lissa's exact opposite in most ways. Dexter was built like a barrel, with bad skin and scarecrow brown hair. His clothes all came from thrift stores by choice, and none of them fit well. He sometimes didn't shower for days, though the smell never really bothered Lissa.

He was also angry. Eternally, endlessly, and ecstatically angry. Angry at school. Angry at his mom who was off God knows where in Afghanistan with the army. Angry at his used-car salesman dad (Yes, dammit, Lissa, he knows you want the Bug! It's the perfect car for a pest!). He'd never seen a television show or movie he liked, but he also never let an opportunity pass to call something new inferior to something old. His smartphone was full of metal and white power punk bands, not that he was any more racist than the next guy. He was just happier when he was angry.

About the only thing he was never really mad at was Lissa. School rumor was they were dating, but it wasn't true. One day last month, Dexter had quietly started holding Lissa's hand, and she gently, but firmly withdrew it without comment. For two days, Dexter took the bus and then reappeared at her side, ranting nonstop about the people he'd seen there as if nothing had ever happened.

Lissa was big on boundaries, and Dexter was even bigger on having someone willing to let him express the art of his rage without judging.

"What is it with you and the car, anyway?" asked Dexter, spitting off to the side of the road and shoving his hands deep into his jeans. "You can drive for hours out of this dump and still not see anything interesting except possibly bestiality. Pretty sure you could find that here if you looked."

Lissa shrugged. "It's for next year, when I'm in college."

"Oh, bullshit," replied Dexter. "You're going to live on campus within walking distance of everything. Plus, I'll bet you dollars to donuts that your dad is planning on getting you a car for graduation anyway. Your parents make bank, but you're busting ass over at the freakin' Kneel and Steal-"

"Woodlake's."

"Pray for my enlightenment. The point is, you go straight to work to save up for a ten-year-old car that was once an opossum's toilet. Why not just wait for the Prius or whatever?"

Lissa listened to the sound of her shoes in the gravel and watched as the world crawled toward her and Dexter.

"I just want to have something, you know?" she said. "I want a place where I can be by myself and not have to listen to anyone but me and music. No matter how low I play songs at home, Mom complains. I want to have the option to go somewhere."

"You're leaving next year and never coming back," said Dexter. "Me, too, assuming the Navy doesn't suddenly get picky. I just don't understand the rush you're in or why you'd pick being a 'Priest in a Box.'"

Explaining how she felt was never Lissa's strong point. She tended to bottle up when confronted. That's why she wanted a car, HER car, so badly. It would be her pod and her barrier against the world and all it expected out of her. Sometimes she felt like a train with her path laid out on rusty rails from which there was no way to alter it.

First, there would be graduation, then college with both her parents close enough to watch her. She'd study business, something sensible, and then one of her parents would likely find her a good introductory position somewhere. After that, she was supposed to get down to the business of finding someone to reproduce with.

It's not that any of that sounded bad, exactly. Lissa was a fundamentally calm and happy person by nature with a pretty low threshold for satisfaction. It's just that the whole thing seemed so planned. Programmed even. The day Dexter's dad put the little blue Beetle in the lot, though, she saw something else.

She didn't really want to escape her fate, but a side trip now and again outside the control of anyone else looked really amazing.

She said none of those things to the boy walking beside her. She just shrugged again and waited patiently for Dexter to fill the rest of the walk home with profanity.

***

After roughly a month at Woodlake's, Lissa felt like she had the routine down to a science. Alonso told her that she was the best deacon he had ever trained, and he'd been helping set up new Woodlake's locations since the chain opened three years ago. Lissa blushed under the praise, even if she did find the weight of his hand from the pat on her shoulder to be a little uncomfortable.

Her manager assured her after her evaluation period was up he would be putting her in for assistant manager and a raise. Lissa mentally began revising her estimates and wondered if she would be behind the wheel by Christmas.

She liked her job a great deal, even if it was still a little odd. She actually did ask Alonso if she could marry people, and she was surprised to learn that she couldn't, but only because she wasn't eighteen yet and couldn't file the legal paperwork. Alonso said he'd married a dozen people so far, about a third of them in the drive-thru of a Woodlake's.

"The church is really seeing the benefit of this sort of accessibility," he said. "There's even talk about doing funerals at some point."

"Don't those have to be done in a licensed funeral home?" asked Lissa. "I'm pretty sure that they do."

"Smart kid," said Alonso. "You're right, but you can have a viewing anywhere, and there's always memorial services for the cremated to think of. The buzz I'm hearing is that Woodlake's wants to partner with Service Corporation International to set up prep and deliver services for bodies. There's probably not really a lot of money in that sort of thing but the branding, Alice, that's the ticket. You make a Woodlake's where you go for all your spiritual matters and you've got a customer for life."

Lissa looked over at the window where an older deacon named Paul was standing in the wide window box praying with a family in a big Ford Excursion.

"You know," said Lissa, "With a little re-arrangement, you could even do a drive-thru viewing. Prop the coffin in the window box like they do in old westerns."

She wasn't even sure if she was joking.

"See!" said Alonso excitedly. "You're getting it. Still haven't come up with a good way to make it so people driving by and people inside could pay their respects, though. Oh well, it's all still in the maybe stage anyway. Break time's over, Alice. Let's get Paul back inside and you in the window."

Lissa went over and waited for Paul to finish up his Soldier Blessing for Mrs. Dvorestsky, who had three different children in three different branches of the armed forces. She'd heard somewhere that the military was big on recruiting people in small towns without a lot of money. It was a good way to entice people to sign up if they thought they could get somewhere better. Mrs. Dvorestsky was crying a little when Paul finished and bought a copy of Reverend James Feist's book *Onward Christian Soldiers* in addition to her thirty dollar donation. Paul thanked her and stepped aside for Lissa to take his place.

Customers like Mrs. Dvorestsky honestly made Lissa very happy and re-affirmed what she liked about her work. Part of her still felt that Woodlake's was a little tacky, but people at her old church used to come to services in baseball caps and shorts all the time. To her, that was at least as tacky as a drive-thru prayer stand.

On the other hand, she wondered if other churches had to deal with people like the jogger who came during her last shift and asked Lissa to bless his large Pepsi Max.

"You want me to bless a drink?" she had asked. "Why? And for what?"

"For the abortions, please," he said in a low voice just above a whisper. "I need you to bless my drink because it has an abortion in it."

"I'm not sure… what?"

"That's where Pepsi gets its taste from," said the man in his conspiratorial whisper, his face flush from exercise and possible mental illness. "About ten years ago, they altered the taste using cells from an aborted baby's fetus so they could make diet drinks that aren't yucky. That's why the government made them take 'Under God' off of their Fourth of July cans. Legally, you can't mention God when there's an abortion involved. Normally, I get a Coke Zero, but the store on the corner was out of them, and I got this. Can you bless it, please?"

Lissa wasn't entirely sure what to do, but the manager on duty, a severe blonde woman named Sheryl, was watching her out of the corner of her eye.

"Well," said Lissa. "We don't really have an abortion prayer, but I could pray for the soul of a lost child and add in a little forgiveness petition over you buying the Pepsi. Would that work?"

"Oh, would you?" said the man happily. "That would be amazing. Thanks!"

Lissa reached over and took the large drink from the man with reverential care. She felt ridiculous, but the whole thing clearly worried him, and that was her job, after all.

"What's your name?" she asked him.

"Dylan."

"Okay… give me your hand, and in the other hand, we'll both hold the cup. Ready?"

Dylan nodded.

"God, it is not in our understanding why you would take a child so soon, but we take comfort in the knowledge that it is part of your plan and that this child rests with you and your son now. Care for - it as we would. Love it as we would. And we shall count the days until we are all reunited in glory with both this child and you.

"Though grief shall darken our hearts, Yours is the path through pain and to salvation. When the scales of the world are righted, we know that we will be together again, and all that was hidden from us will be made clear as day.

"And Lord, please forgive the transgressions of man, who stumbles in his path to righteousness. Whether through folly or weakness, the faithful lean on Your arm to guide them above petty faults. In Jesus' name, amen."

"Amen," said Dylan, who wiped away a tear before fishing forty dollars out of his running sock and handing it to Lissa. "Next time, hopefully, they'll have the Coke Zero, but if not, then I'll be back. I'll ask for you, Alice!"

And with that, Lissa watched the happy Dylan jog out the door and down the street, sipping his drink in total bliss. Sheryl walked up.

"That wasn't bad, Alice," she said. "Not bad at all. You're working out much better than some of the girls Alonso hires."

"Thank you, Sheryl," said Lissa. What the heck did that mean?

***

Two weeks and approximately halfway to her car goal later, Lissa met Nevaeh Chase under less than ideal circumstances.

It was just coming up to closing at 10 p.m. Lissa was manning both the counter and the drive-thru while Sheryl did the closeout paperwork and counted the day's donations. Only one person had been in for the last hour for a brief Prosperity Prayer regarding a new job she was starting tomorrow. Lissa suspected that the woman was honestly just embarrassed because she needed to use the bathroom on the drive through Madisonville, but seemed thankful enough with her five dollar donation and a nice smile for Lissa.

Other than that, Lissa worked on her chemistry homework, waiting for the all-clear to turn out the lights from her boss. Just then, the small bell that indicated a drive-thru customer went off. Lissa closed her book and headed to the window box.

The car that drove up was so black and clean that the pale leather seats seemed to be floating in the dark rather than part of an actual automobile. She didn't recognize the man at the wheel, but Lissa was pretty good at reading people at this point in the work. This man was angry. Really angry, hunched over the steering wheel with his face lined like a wadded up piece of paper. He was wearing a white t-shirt and checkered jammy pants, and by craning her head a little, Lissa saw that he was driving barefoot. Something had gotten him out of the house in a hurry.

Beside him was, Lissa assumed, his wife. She was in a similar state of dress, but Lissa couldn't make out more because she was twisted over her seat, stretching her safety belt to its limit. Her face was obscured by a mane of wild, curly hair as she hissed words into the back seat.

The girl in the back was Nevaeh, and she looked both defiant and miserable.

In as small a town as Madisonville, every kid knows every other kid in their class, even if they aren't really friends. Lissa saw Nevaeh Tuesdays and Thursdays in Chemistry, and last year, they'd had English together. That had been fun because Nevaeh always asked funny questions about the books.

Other than that, they didn't know each other well beyond an occasional "Hi!" and the one time Lissa had emailed some notes to Nevaeh when she'd had a tooth pulled the day before a test. Nevaeh had brought her a big store-bought chocolate chip cookie the next day. It was still in its plastic in her locker, actually, and Lissa wondered briefly if it was still good.

Nevaeh was tall, nearly six feet, but she was also waif-thin to the point that some people thought she might be anorexic. Nevaeh ran with it and wore loose tank tops and tight slacks that accented her boniness. They were good bones, and in the car, Lissa could see that she had the strong, handsome features that her dad would have if he wasn't so pissed off. Her hair was curly like her mom's, but black and cut short so that it flowed around her face like a storm cloud.

At the moment, she was folded up in the back seat with her long limbs tucked and wrapped around her like a spider. Lissa couldn't see her eyes, but her lips were thin and pulled so tight, they were white.

"Welcome to Woodlake's," chirped Lissa. "How can we aid you this evening?"

Nevaeh's mother turned around quick and sat down prim in her seat, staring straight ahead with an almost zombie-like focus. Her dad turned and looked at her with a hard glance.

"Excuse me, but are there any male deacons that could serve us tonight?" he asked.

"I'm so sorry, but no," replied Lissa. It was the first time she'd been asked that. "It's just me and the manager tonight, and she's a - she, too. I can check the schedule to see when a male deacon is working next if you want, but are you sure there's not something I could help you with?"

Nevaeh's dad looked her up and down in a rather intense way that made her wonder what he was thinking.

"This manager," he asked. "Is she pretty? What does she look like?"

"I don't understand why-"

"Would you, please, just answer my question," he hissed. "It's important."

"Okay," said Lissa awkwardly. "Umm, yeah. Sheryl's pretty. She's about thirty, white, big grey eyes. She's in good shape, works out, and has a cute, short bob haircut."

"What color hair"

"Blonde," said Lissa. "Like, I don't know, a Marilyn sort of blonde?"

Where on Earth was all this going? Nevaeh's dad was already shaking his head.

"I guess it will have to be you, then," he said with annoyed resignation. "I don't have anything against women and religion, you understand? That's not what this is about. It's just I would have preferred a man for this."

Lissa waited.

"Do you know my daughter? You're about her age," he asked pointing to the back seat. Lissa gave a little wave.

"Hi, Nevaeh," she said with her professional chirp. "We have Chem together, right? I was just studying when y'all drove up, actually."

"Well, that's what someone should have been doing in her room tonight," he hissed again. His wife looked like she was trying to sink into her seat, and Nevaeh looked off over the dashboard with one eye peering through her mop of hair.

"But that's not what we saw when we walked in to ask her if she had any laundry that she wanted added to the load. No, she was off using the bathroom, and left her computer open and do you know what we saw?"

Lissa was reasonably sure what the answer was going to be but went with a quiet, "No, sir."

"Pornography," he whispered. "And not just any pornography, mind you. It was gay pornography. It was two women doing things to each other. And when I clicked back? It was more and more and more of it. Just video after video and all of it lesbians. My daughter is addicted to lesbian pornography, apparently."

Lissa looked briefly into the back seat and locked eyes (well, eyes and the one eye peering from beneath her hair) with Nevaeh. This was obviously very embarrassing to her, and there was a plea in her glance asking Lissa to not say anything about this at school. Lissa gave just the barest nod before turning back to her father.

"She needs help," he said, some of the edge coming off his voice and true concern coming though. "We drove right over here because, well, you're the only house of God open. Can you pray with her? Show her that this isn't right? Maybe it's best if it's a girl, after all. You can tell her that liking girls - that way - isn't natural. You know that. You work in a place like this, and they wouldn't let you if you were like that."

Lissa wasn't attracted to girls. Truth be told, she wasn't really attracted to anyone that she could think of. She'd seen porn on the internet. Who hadn't? But the videos and images of sex didn't really interest her much. After seeing more than one or two, the whole thing started to become vaguely medical, anyway. She wasn't a prude who thought sex was gross or sinful or anything, but it just never seemed to come up much in her own musings.

She also didn't really feel one way or the other about Nevaeh's attractions either, though for a brief, hysterical moment her brain randomly screamed, "You have a dyke's cookie!" at her and threatened to unleash a horribly inappropriate giggle. She held it in and did her job.

"Okay," said Lissa. "I think that we can help you out tonight. We've got a wonderful resistance to temptation sermon that only takes a minute or two. It's popular with straying spouses, so there's the fleshly aspect of it. I can also add a side of duty and respect for God's path to aid her in focusing on school. That is, if she's willing-"

"She is," said her mother over-loudly. It was the first time she'd spoken.

"Sweetheart?" asked her dad, turning back over the seat. "Will you pray with this nice girl?"

Lissa was certain Nevaeh would rather do anything else in the world, but she also knew, as teenagers often do, that the easiest way to make the parental humiliation stop was to just plow through it as fast as possible.

"Pull forward a little, sir," asked Lissa, and the big, black car inched until the back window was right in front of the drive-thru. Lissa leaned down as the power window was rolled down by Nevaeh's dad. For the first time, the girl in the back seat turned to look at her fully.

"Hey," said Lissa in a coaxing, soothing voice. "Come over here a second." Nevaeh scootched over in the seat. When she got to the window, she swung her long legs up and kneeled. Lissa reached her hands out, and Nevaeh took them. For a second, Lissa looked at her small paws being wrapped in the long, lithe fingers of the other girl and decided to take this sermon just a little further.

"Can you come out the window a little?" she asked, and Nevaeh gently eased her head and torso out of the window of her dad's car. At this angle, the two girls were eye to eye, and Nevaeh looked at Lissa with a sort of frankness that was confrontational, but not otherwise directed at Lissa specifically. It was just this whole, stupid mess.

"Okay," said Lissa. "Repeat after me. Dear God, here at Your feet sit I, unworthy of mercy or love…"

"Dear god, here at your feet sit I… un- unworthy of the mercy of love."

"But through the blood of Your Son, the Redeemer, may I be washed clean."

"But through the blood of your son, the redeemer, may I be washed clean."

"I place my confidence in You, knowing that You will guide me from sin.

"I place my confidence in you… I don't want to do this," whispered Nevaeh.

"It's almost over," said Lissa. "Don't worry. I'm not going to tell anyone. It's okay. Let's just finish it, and we'll go home."

Nevaeh nodded and continued to repeat after Lissa. Her hands squeezed the smaller girl's quite tight, but in this line of work, Lissa was used to passionate grips. If it got too painful, you were supposed to try and get them to grip two fingers instead of your hands. Labor and delivery wards discovered that this cut down on the broken fingers of fathers, according to the training manual.

Suddenly, the lights went out at Woodlake's, and both Nevaeh and Lissa jumped a little. From inside, Sheryl was calling to Lissa and telling her she was locking the door. Lissa shouted over her shoulder that she was with a last-minute customer, and Sheryl leaned against the counter patiently.

When Lissa looked back to Nevaeh, she could no longer make out the girl's features. It was all just wild hair and blank space. Lissa leaned in for the final appeal to walk along God's chosen path, and as Nevaeh repeated it, Lissa whispered, "I don't think you did anything wrong."

Why did I say that? I'm going to get in trouble, she thought?

Nevaeh finished and waited. Her dad tapped her on the thigh. He was holding a twenty for the donation. Nevaeh took it and handed it to Lissa.

"Thank you for staying open late for us," said Nevaeh's father, who had calmed considerably.

"Yeah," said Nevaeh unexpectedly. "Yeah, thanks. I feel a little better about it now."

"I work Monday and Wednesday nights and Sunday days," said Lissa. "If you ever need anything, come on by. Oh, and I'll see you at school, right?

"Tomorrow," said Nevaeh.

With that, Nevaeh let go of Lissa's hands and slid back into the backseat of her dad's car. They drove off past the island of light from the sign and were off into the Texas night.

Lissa put the twenty in the donation box, and Sheryl asked her if she wanted a ride home since it was a little late and on her way. Lissa said yes, gathered her books, clocked out and made it home just as her mother brought water to boil for pasta.

***

The next day, Nevaeh gave Lissa a little smile from across the room, but they didn't sit together or anything. When the bell rang, they neither hurried nor delayed in order to run into each other, but proceeded in their normal rhythms and routines on their way to their next educational gear.

Lissa walked home with Dexter as usual, who had chosen today, for some reason, to wax angrily on the political correctness he felt was being forced upon him by the world.

"It's like this, Lis," he said in that strange street preacher manic way of his. "It used to be a man said what he wanted to say, right? Even if it was unpopular. People respected his right to say it and gave it a fair spot.

"Now, though? You have to watch out because the overly sensitive brigade will come for you through, like, social media and stuff like that. They'll find out your name and where you live, and they'll tell your boss, and they'll mock you and scream until you're blasted from the face of the Earth for even one second daring to say something unpopular."

Lissa looked at him sideways and said nothing. It was just words.

"Like, for instance," he went on. "You can't say a mean thing about anyone gay anymore. Or black. Or even a woman. Just by virtue of them being non-white guys, they get this whole pass on criticism. You say anything, and I mean anything, at all negative about some colon crusher or a rug doctor and then you're some kind of stupid bigot. That's not fair. It didn't used to be that way."

"You've been listening to White Pride again, haven't you?"

"Nah, Skullhead! They knew it long ago. Everyone else can have a damned Pride parade but guys like me. It's discrimination. I'm tired of being told I'm an asshole just because I don't agree with a couple of dudes suing a bakery because it doesn't want to make their Liza Minelli cake."

"Do you ever watch porn on the computer?" asked Lissa out of nowhere, doing the impossible and stopping Dexter in the expression of his hate.

"What does that have to do with the price of action figures on eBay?" he replied.

"Do you?"

"Well, yeah. Sure. I guess."

"Do you ever watch lesbians?" pressed Lissa. "Like, do you ever type, 'lesbians' into a search bar and watch two girls, you know, having sex?"

"I, well, yeah," said Dexter, sort of looking straight ahead now instead of down at Lissa. The whole line of questioning seemed to be making him uncomfortable. "So?"

"How about Asians?"

"For God's sake, Lissa, what are you talking about?" he spat. "Yes. I've watched lesbians going down on each other and I've watched Asian girls in videos specifically because they were Asian. I suppose you think I'm a bigot because of that."

The rest of the walk happened in a sullen silence. Lissa didn't think Dexter was a bigot. Not really. But it was sort of bothering her that he considered people like her to be a category of pornography.

***

Sundays at Woodlake's were brutal these days. The chain had really taken off, with people loving either the convenience of the drive-thru or the one-on-one sermonizing catered to their spiritual needs done in the pray-in area. Gone were the days when you'd dress up and head to church to hear a reverend or priest talk about what he thought you needed to hear about God. Now you got it your way.

The company noticed the Sunday upswings and took immediate action. Lissa was already an assistant manager, and true to his word, Alonso has gone to bat for her at corporate. Fourteen dollars an hour? It seemed like a ridiculous amount of money to her! The little blue Beetle was almost hers, and her mother was looking into the car insurance offered by her company for adding Lissa onto her policy. It was really going to happen.

The mission had become an extremely popular picnic area as well, with nice seating being shipped in for outside and more room being cleared for industrial microwaves so people could heat up their packed lunches. The chain didn't want to sell food because of a regulatory headache, but it did add credit card access to the soda machines and a freezer where you could buy ice. Paper plates and plasticware were given away for free with donations.

Picnickers were encouraged to share their food with the three or four homeless people that occasionally came by looking for a handout. Some of them even did so. If not, the Baptist church down the street gave out donuts and coffee until 11 a.m.

Currently, Lissa was training a new hire by herself. He was a man in his forties named Charles, and while he was happy to have the job, he wasn't particularly pleased by having to answer to a high school girl less than half his age. It seemed to irk him that Lissa called him by his first name, but he knew that it wouldn't do any good to complain.

He was passionate, Lissa gave him that. He wandered a bit from the approved script, too much for her tastes, but he was well-received, especially by the single mothers that came in. In fact, one in particular with a young son was eyeing him right now for service. Lissa was just about to walk Charles over to them when she spied Nevaeh and her mother coming through the doors.

"Charles," she asked. "I think that lady over there is waiting for you especially, and I also think it's time you tried a solo sermon. You up for it?"

110

"Sure," he said. "It's about time, don't you think?"

"Okay, here's what we're going to do," she said. "You sit that lady and her son in booth three, and I'm going to take the woman and teenage girl that came in behind them in booth four. They're regular parishioners of mine. Sit with your back to me so you can tap me on the shoulder if you need anything. Sound good?"

"Is the babysitting strictly necessary by now?" Charles asked condescendingly.

"Trust me," said Lissa. "You never know what you're going to run into in this job. I still ask for help all the time. Go on, now, and good luck."

Charles rolled his eyes a bit as he did what he was told, but he greeted the mother warmly and had a high-five for the boy. Meanwhile, Lissa went over to Nevaeh and her mom.

In daylight, and not frazzled from the excitement of her daughter's unexpected descent into hedonism, Mrs. Chase was quite pretty. She greeted Lissa not with a "Hello," but with an unexpected hug that jostled the girl. Over Mrs. Chase's shoulders, Lissa saw Nevaeh roll her eyes a bit, but she did have another of those little smiles to throw Lissa's way.

"It's nice to see you again," said Lissa. "Welcome to Woodlake's. Can I take you to a seat?'

"Yes, Alice," said Mrs. Chase. "That would be lovely. We're both so glad that you're working today. Aren't we, dear?"

Nevaeh nodded.

They sat in the booth, the Chases on one side and Lissa on the other, half-listening to Charles recite a very basic Sunday sermon for the mother and her boy. He seemed to be doing fine, and Lissa turned her attention to her own parishioners.

"You made quite an impression on Nevaeh the other night," said Mrs. Chase. "She asked if we could start coming here for church now, and we decided to give it a shot. I was a little, you know, hesitant, but there's no arguing with the fact that you were there when we needed you."

"Happy to help," said Lissa, smiling. "I take this job very seriously."

"It's impressive," continued Mrs. Chase. "You're so young, and yet you were the calmest person there that night. You knew just what to say in what must have been a very awkward situation."

"You get over the concept of awkward situations pretty quickly in this line of work," said Lissa. "What would you like today? We've got our weekly special Sunday sermon, of course. It's about forgiveness as taught in Matthew. Or is there something else you need?"

Mrs. Chase looked at her daughter, then replied, "I think we'll take the special, dear."

Lissa began. She liked this week's sermon. Matthew was her favorite of the Gospels because it seemed the kindest to her. She spoke with fervor about the nature of forgiveness between men and how if you could not seek to forgive yourself then you could expect no forgiveness from God.

112

Lissa suspected God didn't really mean that. It was probably just his version of the "I'm not angry, just terribly disappointed" speech.

When she was finished and received another twenty dollar donation from Mrs. Chase, Lissa got up to wish them goodbye, but Nevaeh looked over at her mom with a meaningful glance. Lissa sat back down and asked if there was something else.

"The other night," whispered Nevaeh. "You said you didn't think I had done anything wrong."

Lissa felt her stomach drop but nodded. She was going to lose her job.

"That really meant a lot to me," continued Nevaeh. "I don't know why I started looking at stuff like that. I think I would like to come see you some more. Like, once a week. Would that be okay?"

"Well, sure, I guess," said Lissa. "But why?"

"It was just nice, you know?" said Nevaeh. "I honestly felt like someone was guiding me, forgiving me. It's really silly, I know, but I got more out of holding your hands in the back seat of the car than I've ever gotten out of church."

Lissa felt the double entendre hang in the air, but Mrs. Chase was nodding along.

"She talked about you all day yesterday,' her mom said. "About how you really touched her. I was mad that you told her she hadn't done anything wrong, but I see now that what you were saying was that she hadn't done anything she couldn't come back from. That's so deep. That's just amazing that you can do that. Would it be okay

113

if she came every Thursday night? I'll make sure she has a donation."

Lissa looked at Nevaeh, who was grinning in a strange way. Lissa didn't know what to think. She'd meant it when she said she didn't think Nevaeh had done anything wrong, and not the way her mom believed. On the other hand, she hoped this wasn't some sort of weird ploy because Nevaeh thought Lissa might be interested in her romantically.

In retrospect, holding her hands and whispering in her ear might not have been the best solution at that time. Oh man, what the heck was she going to do?

"I'd be happy to pray with you whenever you like," Lissa told Nevaeh in what she hoped was an adult tone of voice that left no ambiguity. In response, Nevaeh reached over and took Lissa's left hand in both of hers.

"Amen," she said with a glint in her eye. "See you next Thursday."

***

For most of the week, Lissa silently compiled a list of all the people she could talk to about her genuine confusion over the deal she made with Nevaeh and how to handle her if she came Thursday.

Dexter was out. There was zero chance that he wouldn't immediately start making dirty jokes about the subject, and that would definitely just confuse Lissa further. She also felt no desire to know for sure she was actively starring in another person's sex

114

fantasy, which was already sort of the problem she suspected she had now.

Her dad came to mind, but she already knew what he would say on the subject. The born office diplomat, he would tell her to be frank and honest and blah, blah, blah. That was all well and good, but Lissa remembered the anger on Nevaeh's father's face and the strange fear that her mother displayed in the car as opposed to the way she acted out in public in the light of day. That worried her a great deal, and she suspected that no matter what Nevaeh's intentions were, her coming to Woodlake's to see her was probably a good thing in one way or another. Honesty would definitely endanger that, and she wanted to help.

Her mom? Though they weren't nearly as easy and close as Lissa was with her dad, her mom tended to have the most realistic point of view on things. Plus, she was a woman and might get it more.

She didn't want to risk bringing it up with Sheryl or Alonso. Not with her car so close. Two more checks.

It was suddenly depressing to Lissa when she realized how short her list of people was to talk to about something important. She began praying that Thursday would be busy so that the whole thing could be rushed through.

***

It wasn't.

Part of the reason Lissa worked Thursdays was it was slow enough for her to handle on her own now. People preferred to come in on the weekends after payday, though there were always customers. The early evening had started out brisk enough with standard prayers, and one father came in specifically to buy his son the latest in the Noah's Ark themed plush line (it was a kangaroo this week). By 7:30 p.m., though, Lissa leaned against the counter and flipped through a book on Texas history she didn't need to read, but it passed the time in what she felt was a productive manner.

She was actually starting to doze off like Santa Anna at San Jacinto when the bell rang, and Nevaeh came in.

The taller girl walked like a giraffe, head bobbing and arms motionless at her side as she hooked her fingers into the belt loops of her jeans. She was smiling as she came up to the counter where Lissa had laid down her book. Hoping to appear casual, Lissa affected a nonchalant pose and crossed her arms while smiling back.

Look at me, she thought ruefully. I'm a cool kid. This is how cool kids look. Yeeeaaahhhh.

"Hey Lissa," said Nevaeh. She full on hopped up on the counter and looked back into the empty room with her back mostly turned to Lissa. "You busy?"

"It's pretty quiet this time of night," said Lissa. "I mostly do homewo-"

"BALL PIT!" shouted Nevaeh, and before Lissa realized what was going on, she'd vaulted off the counter and ran into the children's area. By the time Lissa followed, Nevaeh had fallen backward into the expansive pool of brightly colored balls and was making snow angels.

Ball angels. Whatever.

"I haven't been in a ball pit since I was a little kid," said Nevaeh with pure, unfiltered happiness. "You know what my favorite part of a ball pit is?"

"The bit where you take off your shoes so that you don't track dirt and bacteria into a place where kids play?" replied Lissa testily.

"Nope," said Nevaeh. She kicked off her shoes at Lissa, who ducked when the sandals went flying past her head and hit the glass wall with a wet-sounding, plastic slap. "What I like, liked, love is when you get out after being in one for about half an hour. You can feel the pressure and the buoyancy of the balls on your skin. It's like phantom limb, but fun. You feel like you're never going to touch the ground again."

Lissa looked on while Nevaeh rolled around in the pit. As she'd told Charles, you see all kinds of things in this job. This was definitely a new one for Lissa.

"Was there something you needed, Nevaeh?" asked Lissa. "I'm pretty sure your mom said she wanted me to pray with you, not dodge your shoes while you acted like a spaz."

Nevaeh crawled over to the edge of the pit. She fished a twenty out of her back pocket and gave it to Lissa. Still in the pit, she looked at Lissa and her assistant manager stance. Even Lissa could tell how ridiculously affected she was, some skinny high school senior trying desperately to be a minister in a drive-thru church. She finally gave up and laughed.

"You just wanted to get out of the house, huh?" said Lissa.

"Pretty much, yeah," said Nevaeh. "Sorry about the act with my mom on Sunday. They really freaked out about the lesbian thing. I don't even think it has anything to do with religion. It's never come up before or anything. They just sort of lost it, and when we came over here, I think they saw the perfect, prim little daughter and decided you'd be a good influence on me."

"I'm not prim," said Lissa. "Yes, I'm little and you're a giant, fine, but I don't understand where all this damned 'perfect doll' crap comes from. Just because I work here doesn't mean I dress my table legs or anything. No one's ever caught me watching porn like you, but I've seen it and didn't die from clutching my pearls too hard around my neck. I'm just trying to save for a car and liked this better than changing sheets at a motel. There's nothing wrong with trying to make money doing something spiritual!"

Lissa was shocked at herself for the outburst. She had no idea what brought it on so strong. Part of it was Nevaeh's flippant attitude about the job and what kind of person Lissa must be for taking it. It was those rails again, the same ones that Lissa's parents laid down. All she seemed to be was a supporting character in other people's lives, background.

She'd spent all week worrying about what to do when Nevaeh came, certain that she needed help and determined to make sure the other girl knew that Lissa was only interested in her as a friend and a professional. All that mental preparation and Nevaeh was about as serious as a puppet show. Nevaeh certainly hadn't expected the reaction she got, and she had the sense to look ashamed about having provoked it.

"Hey," she said. "I'm sorry, okay? I didn't mean anything by it."

Lissa took a deep breath and said nothing.

"Look, it wasn't all an act," said Nevaeh, coming a little closer. "You really were there for me that night. Mom and Dad were nuts, and you calmed them down and got me out of deep trouble. And it really did mean a lot to me that you said I hadn't done anything wrong. I guess I just kind of assumed you were trying to be all piously forgiving and stuff. Like, big medicine woman of the tribe sort of thing. I really did look forward to coming here tonight. We can pray if you want, but I'd like to just hang out in here, too, if that's okay."

Throughout the exchange, cartoon animals were singing songs about friendship on the big TV above the play area. Lissa couldn't take the irony anymore and walked over to shut it off. When she looked back, Nevaeh was still waiting with an earnest look on her face. Lissa sat on one of the couches where parents could watch their kids.

"Yeah," she said. "It's okay. I don't know what that was all about. This job gets to you sometimes."

"Are we friends, like, then?" asked Nevaeh. Lissa smiled.

"Yeah, we're friends," said Lissa.

"Then come play in the ball pit with me!" said Nevaeh, and tumbled backward again, her legs flipping up into the air. Colored balls flew everywhere, and Lissa shook her head as she heard the drive-thru bell go off. She left Nevaeh to her game.

The man in the car was drunk, and Lissa had a hard time understanding him. She wasn't sure what he wanted because the only things she caught in his slurring were the name Carol and the word "nigger." Lissa just nodded along until the man said thank you and drove away, jumping the curb on the way out.

When Lissa went back into the children's area, she didn't see Nevaeh. Maybe she was up in the tube maze or something. No, there was the purple of her tank top. She'd just buried herself completely in the pit.

"What's the prayer going to be?" came her muffled voice.

"Are you still joking around, or do you really want to do this?" asked Lissa. "I don't want to start something and have you mess me up in the middle."

"I swear to God and Jesus and all His angels that I want to hear your schtick. Your last one was good, and my parents paid good money for this."

"But you're not going to come out of there, are you?" asked Lissa.

"Nope. I like it here. Get to preachin'. The customer is always right, and the customer wants to hear a sermon while she's in her ball pit."

Lissa sat on the edge of the pit, and thought for a second, then started speaking to where she vaguely figured Nevaeh's head was.

"Long ago, there was a great city in what is now Iraq. And it was the greatest city in the world, so large that it took three days to walk across it. Its name was Nineveh."

Nevaeh actually popped her head out suddenly.

"Come again?" she said.

"Nineveh," said Lissa. "Its name was Nineveh."

Nevaeh laid back but did not submerge herself again. Lissa continued.

"Nineveh was beautiful and rich. Its people were prosperous and happy, but in their prosperity, they forgot the will of God. They took to worshipping their own success and cleverness, and God decreed that He would destroy the city. However, He gave them one chance.

"God spoke to Jonah, an Israelite, and told him that Jonah should travel to Nineveh and preach of the coming destruction from the Lord if they did not repent, fast, and pray. If they did so, they would be spared.

"Nineveh was an ancient enemy of Israel, and Jonah had no desire to see the city saved, will of God or no. So Jonah fled from his mission, knowing that God loved him and would forgive him for his weakness and anger."

"This is where he gets eaten by a whale, right?" asked Nevaeh.

"A big fish," said Lissa. "The Bible specifically says a big fish."

"But weren't you guys selling a play set last week with a killer whale that was all about Jonah, and-"

"Nevaeh!"

"Okay, sorry," she said. "Carry on."

"They pick up those rubber figures from toy company liquidations, I think," said Lissa. "Anyway, yes. Jonah fled to the sea, but the sea was wild and stormy. Jonah was cast into the water and swallowed by a big fish.

"For three days Jonah fasted and prayed in the belly of the fish until he was spit back out again onto the shore. Repentant and fearful, Jonah obeyed the Lord and went to the wicked people of Nineveh to declare His doom."

"What happened to the city?" asked Nevaeh. Despite herself, she was riveted. Lissa was a gifted storyteller, and Nevaeh could see the roiling seas and the fear in Jonah's eyes when she closed her own to picture them. She knew the basic story, of course, but nothing much beyond the fact that someone had pissed off God and sent a whale to eat them as a kind of celestial time out.

As Lissa spoke, she saw the city of Nineveh, imagining spires and a huge multi-colored population walking around in splendid robes, all ignorant of the will of God that was considering their deaths and testing that consideration on a single man and his hate and terror.

"Jonah came to the city, and he began to speak to the people there. He told them of God's boundless mercy. He told them that though they were good and wealthy and had everything that they could want, that they were cruel to Israel and forgetful of the God who gave them such abundance.

123

"The people of Nineveh heard the words of Jonah, and they did indeed repent, and fast, and pray. God stayed His wrath, and the city of Nineveh continued for hundreds of years as a beacon of hope and light to the world.

"But Jonah was angry with God for sparing the city, hating the people of Nineveh as much as ever. His heart was small, and he was unable to extend the love of God for His people to others. That was why the fish was sent to swallow him.

"In the end, mercy and understanding for those you don't know or who have hurt you is hard, but as it is, it is the will of God that we try."

Nevaeh was quiet as Lissa finished the tale of Jonah. She'd worked on it all week.

"Why doesn't anyone tell the story like that?" asked Nevaeh. "You hear about Jonah and the whale your whole damned life, and nobody ever tells it like that."

Lissa shrugged. "Most of the real rules in the Bible are hard. It's easier to avoid shellfish and be angry at gays than it is to offer salvation to a city full of people that have been your enemy since before you were born. Folks like the Jonah and Noah stories because they make good cartoons."

Nevaeh said nothing.

"I need to turn out the lights and do the till and stuff," said Lissa. "Do you want to leave or wait?"

"I'll wait and walk with you," said Nevaeh. "Is there anything I can do to help? Like, wipe down counters or something like that?"

"You can pick up the balls you spilled," said Lissa. "And there's glass cleaner and paper towels in that closet if you want to do the windows real quick."

Nevaeh hopped out of the pit, more carefully this time so as to not spill any more balls, and started cleaning while Lissa did the close out. Thirty minutes later, Woodlake's was clean and locked, and the lights were turned off. The two girls stood outside of the darkened building, and after some discussion, began both walking in the same direction toward home.

"You know something weird?" said Lissa after listening to nothing but the grind of gravel under their shoes for a full minute.

"I know a lot of weird things," said Nevaeh. They moved in and out of the pools of light from street lamps, and it made her pale face look like it was going through a sped-up cycle of the moon's phases. "Tell me your weird thing, and I'll tell you if I know it.'

"Woodlake's is the first ball pit I've seen since I was very little," said Lissa. "Even places like McDonald's and Chick-Fil-A that have playgrounds don't have ball pits anymore. You don't even see them at state fairs. We're, like, the only one that does it still. I wonder why that is."

"Oh, I know this one!" said Nevaeh. "Mom used to work as a health inspector. Aside from the church thing, what's the biggest difference between Woodlake's and the other places you've named?"

Lissa didn't know.

"Food," said Nevaeh. "You don't serve food, and you don't allow food in the play area. I saw the sign. Back in the 'seventies and eighties, whenever they'd empty ball pits in fast food joints, they almost always found, like, rotting chicken nuggets and stuff like that at the bottom. A bunch of kids got sick that way.

"So that means there are all those people that make ball pit stuff suddenly not having anyone using them because they end up being rainbow petri dishes. Your bosses come in and buy up all that stuff super cheap, and there you go. Just like the toy liquidations for Jonah's whale."

Listening to Nevaeh go on was nothing like listening to Dexter's rants on the road. Nevaeh talked in a somewhat annoying way that included way too many instances of the word "like," but there was an inclusiveness in her manner that Lissa didn't even know she was missing in conversation. She was being talked with, not at.

It was nice.

The two girls stopped at a stop sign. Lissa's house was another half mile along the street while Nevaeh's was down into the subdivision.

"I'm glad you came in tonight," said Lissa. "It was fun."

"Yeah," agreed Nevaeh. "Surprisingly, it was. Same time next week?"

"I'll be there," said Lissa. "And I'll see you at school, too."

Nevaeh waited a moment and said, "Can I hug you? Are we, like, friends that hug?"

"Okay," said Lissa. Nevaeh bent down and rested her chin on Lissa's shoulder, putting her arms around her. Lissa placed both hands on the taller girls' shoulder blades, leaning forward into the embrace like old people do. It was only for a moment, but it was long enough for Lissa to wonder when she'd last been hugged by anyone besides her parents.

Nevaeh stood up, looked at Lissa for a second, then waved and turned away. Lissa was relieved to see her go. Nevaeh was cool, but she was exhausting, and Lissa was still afraid that Nevaeh was going to try and kiss her or something.

It was fun tonight, though. Lissa walked on toward home, passing her blue Bug on the way. Very soon there wouldn't be any walking at all.

***

Dinner was red beans and rice because Lissa's mom could make it by throwing everything in a rice steamer and forget about it until her daughter got home. As they ate, Ms. Liu grilled her daughter about her plans.

"You've been saving up your money really well," she said. "But what are you actually going to do once you get the car? You know you're still going to have your curfew, right? This isn't an excuse to just drive around all night."

"I know," said Lissa between bites. "I'll still be coming and going at the same time, I'll just be doing it a bit faster is all."

"I mean it, sweetheart," said her mom. "Your grades are important, and things get out of hand when kids go joyriding recklessly."

Joyriding, Lissa sniggered to herself at the archaic term. God forbid she go joyriding. What if she ran into some reprobates that forced her to take reefer madness? She hid her smile by chewing. Ms. Liu sighed.

"I still don't know why you can't go to the University of Dallas," said Lissa's mom. "They'll accept you, surely, and you'd be close enough to still live here."

"Mom, it's a two-hour commute," said Lissa. "I'd never do anything but drive, study, and sleep."

"I'm just worried that you're not considering your responsibilities," said Ms. Liu. Lissa had no idea what the hell that meant.

***

It was two weeks later. Nevaeh, true to her word, had come in every Thursday, and even on Monday this week to pray and hang out with Lissa. It was a strangely easy friendship, though Lissa felt weird about essentially charging Nevaeh for the privilege. When she said something, Nevaeh waved it away. It was her parents' money, and they had no real lack of it.

They'd begun talking together in school as well, sitting next to each other in Chemistry and occasionally sharing lunch. Lissa's fear that Nevaeh or anyone else would think they were dating seemed kind of silly now. Surprisingly, Dexter began joining them as well, something Lissa worried about. The two were extremely opposite personalities, but no matter how passionate either got in their speech, they were cordial enough.

After school on Thursday, the three of them walked towards Woodlake's. For the most part, Lissa was content to listen to them argue, and only occasionally joining in.

Today, they were arguing about death.

"Death is a sucker's game," spat Dexter. "Not dying. Dying's just natural. I'm talking about the business of death. All that funeral home shit. Do you know what that freakin' costs? More than a new car sometimes, and that's just for the basic set-ups. All so folks can look at a corpse that's hollowed out and filled with diapers to prevent leaking while everyone cries. It's the most expensive two hours anyone will ever spend. I'm not having any of that mess."

"Why would you care?" asked Lissa. "You'd be dead."

"Maybe I believe in an afterlife," he said. "Maybe I just don't want someone to have to pawn things so they can afford to wrap my ass up like a Christmas present no one will ever open. When I'm dead, I don't want anything. No wake. No box. Either burn me to ash or dump me in the sea. Either way, I want off this damned rock within forty-eight hours."

"Funerals are for the living, though," said Nevaeh.

"Who do you think I'm considering here?" he retorted.

"People want to say goodbye," replied Nevaeh. "They need it. You ever, like, see people whose kids go missing, and then some reporter talks to them years later and there's still no answer? They're haunted. Sometimes they have funerals with no bodies at all, just to have the symbolism. It's closure."

"I think I'd like a funeral," said Lissa. "I believe in Heaven, and I can't imagine how sad it would be to look down and see that no one cared to say goodbye."

"If you're going to spend eternity worrying about that, it's going to be a long death," said Dexter.

"I want, like, a Viking funeral," said Nevaeh.

Lissa and Dexter looked up at the girl questioningly.

"When Vikings died, they'd put them on a boat with the weapons of their fallen enemies," she said. "Then they'd push the boat off, set it on fire with an arrow, and watch the boat burn until it collapsed into the water. That was how they entered Valhalla, mead hall of heroes."

"That. Is metal," said Dexter. "Nice if you can afford it."

"Agreed," said Lissa. "But I'll stick with the regular American burial customs."

"Vikings came to America," said Nevaeh and Dexter together.

Lissa shrugged. They'd reached Woodlake's. It was crowded for a Thursday. Nevaeh was headed home to eat dinner, and then she'd be back up for close. Dexter said he might come up as well. Lissa went inside to change, leaving Nevaeh to warn Dexter that if he made fun of Lissa's prayers, she would personally prove the existence of Hell using nothing but a sharp pencil and a staple remover.

* * *

The engine hiccupped once and then roared into life. Lissa squealed with joy and clapped her hands. The blue Beetle purred like a kitten, and if it did have the faintest odor of animal urine, it wasn't anything that some air fresheners and rides with the windows down couldn't fix.

Lissa made a big show of adjusting the seat and mirrors to suit her. She had to ram the seat all the way to the front, but once she did, the pedals felt made for her feet. She looked over at the dashboard radio and quickly set the exact time. There wasn't much radio worth listening to out here, but she'd set her presets later. She couldn't stop grinning.

Dexter's dad leaned into her window. He was a casual, happy man that came across a little sleazy, but he liked Lissa and had played her straight on the car. After getting updates from her mother on the steady, reliable progress of her savings, he'd quietly done a lot of extra work to ensure she would get plenty of mileage out of the Beetle.

"How's she feel?" he asked Lissa.

"Great!" she said. "Oh my God, it's fantastic!"

Off to the side, Dexter and Nevaeh watched their friend. Even Dexter smiled at Lissa's unbridled enthusiasm.

"You kids hop in there, and let Lissa take her around the block a few times," said Dexter's dad. "I want to make sure everything's acceptable."

"Shotgun!" yelled Nevaeh, and sprinted around the front of the car. Dexter slouched to the back, leaning forward between the seats.

Seatbelts clicked on, and Lissa backed her car out of the lot. With a happy beep of the horn, she carefully started to drive.

Mine, thought Lissa. It's mine. I bought this. I worked for it. I paid for it. I can go anywhere I want. I can drive right out of town if I want. I can drive right out of the country if I want. I'm not going to, but I can if I want.

It was all she'd ever hoped for.

"The silence is deafening," said Nevaeh. "Dex?"

Dexter reached up, handed Nevaeh three packages, and said, "Merry Kwanzaa."

Lissa glanced over. Nevaeh was unwrapping the packages. Inside were three burned CDs with handwritten labels.

"We went through your Spotify account the other night," said Nevaeh. "We decided to honor your increased mobility by breaking your favorite songs, augmented by contributions from your learned friends, into three distinct categories most appropriate to celebrate this occasion."

"Did you swallow a dictionary or something?" asked Dexter.

"Shut it," said Nevaeh. "You've got no drama in your soul. Here we have *Teenage Car Songs*, everything from the Beach Boys to Fastball to Tracy Chapman. Next up is *Teenage Love Songs*, where we find out that Dexter Byron Lilley is a secret superfan of the sappier side of the Beatles. Finally, we offer *Teenage Death Songs*, an ode to those that leave us behind too soon."

"I was outvoted when I suggested Teenage Fuck Songs," said Dexter.

"I voted for you in absentee," said Nevaeh. "What do you want to start with?"

"*Car Songs*," said Lissa. "To be played at maximum volume."

Nevaeh slipped the disc from its package, pushed it into the player, and turned the knob all the way to the right. A driving drumbeat exploded out of nowhere, and the rough, but soft voice, of Bob Seger began explaining the joys and sorrows of Hollywood nights. This was one of her dad's favorite songs, and she remembered every word.

"They drove for miles and miles on those twisting, turning roads," he crooned. "Higher and higher and higher they climbed."

Lissa was only doing forty miles per hour on a residential street in Madisonville, Texas, but she felt every lyric in every single atom of her being. On the center console next to her, Dexter tapped out that staccato drum rhythm with pinpoint accuracy and an absurd look of serenity. Nevaeh leaned her head out the window of the car and her hair blew back from her face as she sang. Lissa looked at her; for the first time, there was nothing obscuring her face, and her eyes were bright as they stared into the setting Texas sun.

***

"These films have a very schizo spiritual message," said Dexter.

He, Lissa, and Nevaeh were sitting together, eating from a tin of cold popcorn and bags of chips, sipping Gatorade and soda. Their backs were to the door of Lissa's Beetle. Ahead of them on the screen, the Peanuts gang celebrated Christmas on the side of the school gym. Showing the three big Charlie Brown holiday specials

133

in the parking lot was an annual community event. They could barely hear the dialogue all the way in the very back of the lot, but they could still read the subtitles and had been watching them since before any of them could remember anyway.

"Here's where we learn if Lissa has somehow been a positive influence on you, I guess," said Nevaeh with her mouth full.

"No, I'm serious," he said. "This is kind of bothering me that I've never noticed it before."

"Noticed what?" asked Lissa.

"Alright," he began. "So *A Charlie Brown Christmas* is like the most mainstream Christian movie ever, right? It's this big celebration of the birth of Christ in a non-pushy sort of way mixed in with a healthy dose of 'don't commercialize and the true meaning of Christmas', and can we just thank Satan it's short for a minute?

"But then you've got the *Great Pumpkin*. That's Linus with this really sincere religious belief totally enduring in the face of persecution only to be rewarded with nothing at the end of it. It's basically the exact opposite of the speech he gives at Christmas. Everyone loses their minds because Christmas is commercial and it should be about faith and togetherness, but when he sits in the pumpkin patch, all the non-believer kids get candy and have a great time without him. I mean, am I missing something here? Lissa? This is your department."

Lissa stared at the screen watching the Nativity play, wheels turning.

"Like, what about Thanksgiving?" asked Nevaeh.

"No one cares rat balls about Thanksgiving, Chase," he said. "Can we all just stay focused on the topic at hand for a second? I'm waiting to be told I'm a genius."

"You're a genius," said Lissa. Nevaeh and Dexter's mouths dropped.

"No really," she said. "That's a good point. If you watched them in the other order, and I guess, technically, we do with just a ten-month break in between, it's all about a little boy having his faith broken and going crazy. I never really gave it much thought, either."

***

Lissa woke for her last week of school before the Christmas holidays set in and snuggled warmly under three mismatched blankets. It was truly getting cold now, and she loved the feeling of her body heat bouncing back and forth under the layers making her toasty. Lissa liked the grey skies of winter but hated to be cold. It was not unusual for her to wear two coats. Dexter mocked her and asked her if she was attempting to make herself look bigger to scare off predators.

Finally awake, she went to the bathroom, did what needed doing, and emerged pretty put together. It was Monday, so she made sure to pack her change of clothes in her backpack, folded neatly into a large freezer bag and labeled with her name. Her mom left for work an hour before Lissa needed to get up, so the house was empty. She microwaved some leftover bacon real quick, stuffed it into a sandwich wrapped in a paper towel along with a banana, and headed to the car with a can of Pepsi Max.

135

Yum, yum, abortion, she thought. Poor weird jogger dude.

Outside, she was surprised to see Dexter wasn't already there. He usually waited sitting on the porch swing for her. She checked her phone to see if she was running later than she thought, but no, she was right on time. Maybe he was sick or slept in. She got in the car and cranked up the heat while she scarfed her breakfast down. When he hadn't appeared by the time she was wiping the crumbs away, she decided to go on ahead. Either he'd left early for some reason and she'd pick him up walking, or he wasn't coming at all. For all his faults, Dexter considered punctuality a point of honor.

Heading down the street, she listened to *Teenage Death Songs*. It was a great sad morning mix. Katie Herzig was on now, baby-voiced and soft as she asked questions about walking through walls. Lissa wasn't convinced this tune was about death. She thought it sounded like a girl afraid to tell someone she loved them, but Nevaeh and Dexter had both told her she was wrong.

Up ahead, she saw the flashing lights of a police car and an ambulance. There was an accident at the stop sign, and she saw some sort of expensive sedan with a huge dent parked jaggedly in the dirt on the side of the road. Lissa hoped everyone was okay, and thoughtfully lowered her speed to twenty miles per hour as she passed the accident, just like they taught her in driver's education.

As she passed the police cruiser and the wrecked vehicle, she spared a brief look at where some people were standing, and her blood turned to ice.

With a screech of her brakes, she almost crashed into a light pole as she pulled off and bolted from the door. Everything turned to slow motion. When she was little, Lissa had nightmares about running away from some sort of terrible monster, but her movements were like she was mired in mud, and the beast behind her was just coming and coming and coming. This was the nightmare all over again, except this time the monster was up ahead.

A woman holding a screaming toddler was crying and yelling at a Texas Highway Patrolman, pointing up and down the street. On the ground, two paramedics desperately compressed someone's chest before finally shaking their heads and standing. As they did so, Lissa got a hard look at what had made her stop.

Dexter was on his knees, his flannel shirt covered in blood. She'd never seen anything so obscene as the naked panic and pain in his eyes when he looked up into Lissa's as she ran toward him. Between them, Nevaeh lay crumbled and broken, her hair matted to her head with blood. There was a scarlet trail from the road to here where Dexter had grabbed her and pulled her out of the traffic. She was so big and tall in life, and now she looked smaller than Lissa. One eye was closed, and the other stared up to heaven.

Something terrible welled up in Lissa's chest, an agony almost too much to bear. Behind that was a screaming rage about the unfairness of it all.

You take it back, God, she thought. You take it back right fucking now, you hear me? I'm a deacon! I AM A DEACON, and I demand you take this back!

God did not take it back.

In the second that became unavoidable knowledge, Lissa let out a wail so loud it sent scared birds flying from the telephone wires. Dexter stumbled to his feet, and for the first time, the two friends fell into each other's arms as Lissa's legs let go. Dexter's own tears finally came like rain, and the grey sky above simply looked down on them with omnipresent indifference. What were a few souls among billions to the Mighty above?

***

"You're going to be here, anyway," said Alonso.

Lissa could not believe the conversation she was having in the manager's office was not some kind of prank in very poor taste. For reasons she couldn't even adequately explain, she'd called Woodlake's shortly after they took Nevaeh's body away and told them what happened. They told her to take the day off, and she could work Tuesday instead. In her grief-addled brain, that sounded very generous and understanding. Now, she realized it was monstrous.

It was nothing, though, compared to what was being discussed right at this moment. She'd arrived early so she could tell Alonso that she would probably be unavailable for some day that week to go to Nevaeh's funeral once it was scheduled, and Alonso dropped his bombshell.

Woodlake's was now officially in the funeral and viewing business. The final approvals were made last week, and though they weren't advertising it yet, the chain was eager to try one out. The Madisonville mission would be the first, thanks to the phone call

Nevaeh's mother had made this morning. Her daughter had so loved her prayer meetings at Woodlake's, by any chance could they have a wake there? Eager to be a trailblazer in the church, Alonso sold them on a full package.

This Thursday, Lissa was expected to work this important occasion.

"C'mon, Alice," said Alonso. "All the managers are going to be there to help. It's our first one. Mrs. Chase specifically asked for you because you were such a good deacon when they would come by, and we're going to need all hands on deck for this. You were going to go a funeral, anyway, so this isn't any different."

"I was going to go to a funeral to mourn!" shouted Lissa. "I wasn't going there to get paid. Nevaeh was my friend. I don't want to work her funeral. I want to say goodbye."

"Okay, first? Don't shout at me," Alonso said sternly. "I'm still your boss, and you need to show me the proper respect. You're understandably upset, so I won't write you up for it this time. However, this is your job, and I'd hate to see your rather remarkable employment here come to an end because you refuse to do it."

Lissa was so shocked she couldn't speak. Fired? For this?

Alonso stood up and came over to her. He hugged her tightly, which Lissa didn't want and immediately hated. She was afraid to say anything, though.

"Look at it like this," he said, patting her back too hard. "You were her friend, but you were also her spiritual adviser. You guided her soul. This is an honor to be doing that one last time. You should be grateful for the opportunity. Plus, management says that we'll get time-and-a-half for funeral work."

Lissa was finally allowed to withdraw from the embrace and look up at her boss. She liked her job a lot, and she felt important in it. This was too much, though. She was only seventeen. She'd just lost her best friend. She was supposed to hide in her room and cry and throw things and remember, not get up and go to work and school and guide souls and whatever like it hadn't even happened. Who could honestly expect her to go on like this?

They do, came her answer in her head. They expect it.

Lissa sighed a long, dead-sounding sigh, and looked down at the floor. She'd drank abortions, and yesterday she swore at God. She was being punished. Eventually, she just nodded, afraid that if she spoke she'd burst into tears.

"Good," said Alonso. "Now, go ahead and clock in. You'll work a little later, but right now, we have some videos on the new funeral protocols that I need you to watch, and then there's a test to take."

Lissa nodded again and sat down while Alonso queued up the videos. There was the brown-haired man in his too sharp contrast again. Alonso left her, and Lissa watched. She watched, and took notes, and was a good girl.

Later that night, when she was the last one in Woodlake's, she buried herself completely in the ball pit and screamed until her throat bled.

***

140

Thursday. Lissa drove as fast as she could so she wouldn't be late for her shift. She most certainly and absolutely did not, in any way, want to do this, but the sooner she started it, maybe the sooner it would end. Dexter sat next to her, spouting hyphenated and increasingly outlandish swears and accusations of sexual deviancy at the tie he was trying to tie. Every few seconds, he would look up an instructional video on his phone and stare at it with a look of intense simian concentration on his face, then give it another go. Lissa was in her uniform, and the only thing that marked this as a different day was the black wristband the company had sent over.

Dexter achieved something like a presentable knot just as they were pulling into the parking lot and shrugged into an old, black suit jacket that had belonged to his uncle. They parked around the back of the building. Lissa came around the car to give him a once over, adjusted his tie and brushed off some lint.

"How's my makeup?" she asked.

"Hell if I know," he said. "You look prettier than you do without it. That's about all the fashion advice I have."

"Just tell me if the liner is straight or running or anything," she said shortly. Dexter made a show of checking thoroughly and declared it look straight to him. With a deep breath, they walked to the entrance.

Outside the door was a stand-up chalkboard sign, the kind you see outside of coffee houses in big cities. On it was written "Neveah Chase, Now She Dwells Above."

They spelled her name wrong, thought Lissa. I don't want to do this here.

"Wait," said Dexter. "Isn't her name spelled-"

"I'll get them to fix it," she interrupted. "Find a place to sit. I need to clock in."

Woodlake's was really trying to make this something memorable. The large picture of Christ adorning the back wall had been draped with black streamers, and black balloons were tied to the booths. Thankfully, the company had been too cheap to personalize them, so they didn't bear a misspelled name. The music in the main room was still contemporary Christian pop, but strictly slower, ballad material to show reverence. The TV in the play area was off, and on a small table stood a sign-in book surrounded by candles and pictures of Nevaeh.

There, next to the drive-thru window box, was the wooden casket with her friend's body. It was elevated enough so that people in the drive-thru lane could see it if they wanted to.

This is so damned wrong, she thought.

"There you are," said an unexpected voice that made her jump. Sheryl was walking up briskly to her. "Go ahead and clock in. This doesn't start for another half hour, so there's plenty of time for you to pay your respects before the rest of her family and friends get here. I know you guys knew each other."

"Yeah," said Lissa with a hitch. "We were pretty close."

"I'm really sorry for your loss," said Sheryl. Lissa was sure she meant that, but she wasn't sure that Sheryl meant it enough. "This might be tough on you, but this is the job we have to do. You up to speed on the procedures?"

Lissa recited them back perfectly. There wouldn't be a group service. Woodlake's didn't do that sort of thing. It was still the same one-on-one service they were known for. Her job, along with the other deacons, was simply to guide mourners, pray with them from the approved list downloaded and printed out on Tuesday, and just, in general, do what they always did.

"And don't forget to ask them if they are here for the viewing first," said Sheryl.

"Why else would they be here?" asked Lissa.

"Same reasons they always come here, I guess," said Sheryl.

"Wait, are we open during this?" said Lissa shocked.

"Of course we are," said Sheryl with a funny look at her assistant manager. "McDonald's doesn't close the whole restaurant for a birthday party. This is a normal business day otherwise. Don't worry, though. I've told everyone that you're to handle most of her people because you were close. Leave the rest to us. Oh, and you don't have to close tonight, either. I'm happy to do it as a favor to you."

Sheryl patted Lissa on the shoulder and walked away. For a moment, Lissa literally could do nothing but stand like a statue. From a far corner, Dexter stared at her with incredulity. He wasn't a dumb guy by any means, but he was still pretty sheltered living out here in the middle of nowhere. Right now, he was taking what Woodlake's was doing to Lissa and comparing it to pretty much everything he had ever complained about. He was hard-pressed to come up with anything worse than this. He felt like he might actually throw up.

Lissa grasped her father's cross for a moment, drawing a little strength. Then she looked at Dexter and nodded. He got up to join her, utterly silent. He reached down to take Lissa's hand and she accepted it with a squeeze that hurt. They walked to the casket and looked.

Lissa had never seen Nevaeh in a dress before, and the one they chose suited her poorly. It was too prim and she never wore blue in life. The long sleeves and the high neckline made her look like something from *Big Love* or like she'd stepped out of a picture from a cult compound. Lissa supposed that maybe the dress was masking the damage the car had done to her body, but it still felt wrong.

When she thought of Nevaeh, it was thoughts of a girl utterly at home in her skin. She loved her odd, bony body and imposing height. Even in winter she'd shed her coat the second she got in the school building. Capri pants and tank tops and belly shirts. Nevaeh used her skin like it was a fashion accessory.

At least they left her hair right, thought Lissa. It was brushed away from her face, but it was still the same lonely storm cloud there on the pillow.

Lissa wasn't sure what to do. This wasn't just the first funeral she was working. It was the first funeral she'd ever been to, period. Nevaeh was the first body she'd ever seen. Her mom should be here with her or something.

She stared at the somewhat plastic face of her dead friend. She glanced at Dexter for a cue, but he, too, was simply looking into the coffin. To Lissa's surprise, he began speaking.

"Nev - I didn't really know you very well," he said. "We'd only been hanging out for, like, a month or two. But it was a good month. Or two, and I thought we were going to have at least a few more months after that. I'm really sorry we didn't, but I'm also really glad I met you. That's all, I guess. I'm just glad I met you, and I'm sorry you're gone."

He didn't cry, but his voice caught just the once in the beginning. It was a short speech, and gruff, but it was one of the kindest things Lissa had ever heard him say. She didn't know what to add, and they stood there for a long time. Lissa was starting to worry that she'd run out the clock before the guests started arriving and still have not said anything. She'd open her mouth and then close it again. She wanted to touch Nevaeh's hand or something, but she was afraid it would be cold and stone-like, and she wasn't sure she could handle that.

"I-"

"Lissa!"

She turned around to see Mrs. Chase coming toward her with another of those jolting embraces that for one second she thought was going to push her back into the casket. Behind her was Nevaeh's father in a blue suit, looking pained and lost.

"So glad that we were able to arrange this here," said Mrs. Chase. "You were so good to Nevaeh. She talked about you all the time and all the things you were teaching her at her prayer meetings. It was the best money we'd ever spent. I would never have believed that someone so young could straighten her out like that, but you're just a marvel. A marvel. God bless you."

"Thank you," said Lissa, pulling back. She wasn't thinking about prayers at the moment. Her mind was flashing through scenes with her friend. Chasing each other through the playground tube maze one night after close. Sitting at lunch and Nevaeh making Lissa spit out her drink with telling dirty jokes about a group of cheerleaders at another table. Dexter and Nevaeh arguing about metal bands over Lissa's head while they walked. Driving. Just the three of them driving around after the sun set, not going anywhere, but using it as an excuse to talk and laugh and be.

Dexter was right. It wasn't a long time, but it was a great time. All Nevaeh's parents could see right now was her as a walking Sunday school for their wayward daughter. It didn't seem to occur to anyone but Dexter that Lissa was deep in her own mourning and could maybe use someone to lean on as well.

Clearly, she wasn't going to get it from the Chases. Nevaeh's father walked up and offered his hand. Lissa shook it and was surprised to feel something pressed into her palm. It wasn't the first time a man had passed her money that way for her work. She imagined that it made them feel slick and gentlemanly. Nevaeh was always a little creeped out by the gesture. In some weird way, it made her feel like a prostitute.

"You've done a lovely job here," he said to her. Lissa nodded, and they moved past her to view their daughter. Lissa looked at her hand. There was a neatly folded one-hundred dollar bill in her palm. She could see the words, "In God we trust" written small on it. She tucked the bill into the back pocket of her slacks, set her face and walked over to greet the next mourners.

At first, Dexter shadowed her. He was thinking that the best thing for him to do was to be by Lissa's side as a sort of shoulder to lean on. Quickly, though, it became apparent that this wasn't really working out. The people who would stop and listen to the prepared prayer would dart their eyes at Dexter and his ill-fitting, secondhand clothes. He looked largely out of place in this gleaming, modern setting and stood out like a sore thumb next to Lissa's carefully constructed corporate perfection. After the third group, he told Lissa he was going to go sit in the back and wait for her.

Lissa nodded, and Dexter saw her teeth were clenched behind her smile.

"It's only an hour and a half more," he said. "You can do it."
She nodded.

For the next hour, Dexter watched people like he'd never watched them before. They drove to Woodlake's in SUVs and freshly washed cars. They wore clothes with a weird informality to them. Their casual button-down shirts and simple dresses probably cost as much as all the clothes he owned combined, but few were wearing suits, veils, or black. It was like they were subconsciously telling people that this was a high-class, but casual, outing. Dexter

147

thought it was a little blasphemous, and that wasn't a word he'd ever sincerely applied to anything before.

A local news station showed up somewhere in the middle. Funerals at a drive-thru church? How novel. Nevaeh's parents were interviewed, and the news van went through the drive-thru lane once to get a glimpse of the body and have Lissa recite the company prayer. Dexter could see her hands shaking, but she was holding it together through sheer force of her incredible will.

The sudden media attention sent Sheryl, Alonso, and most of the other employees preening for the cameras. The plan for Lissa to minister to Nevaeh's mourners was apparently forgotten. Alonso made it a point to press the hands of Nevaeh's redheaded lab partner in between his own meaty palms, praying loudly and feverishly. Even Sheryl, usually cool and collected, was in a performance mood. She would gather folks in small circles and make petitions to God toward rest and peace for Nevaeh's soul. Everyone here was hoping to make an appearance on TV, and perhaps move up in the hierarchy of the church.

Lissa leaned against the wall in the drive-thru, and this time Dexter did go over to her. He was about to ask if she was okay when the bell went off for a customer. Mr. King drove up in his lime green Toyota with a scowl on his face.

"Welcome to Woodlake's," said Lissa. "How can I help y-"

"What's the hold up here?" Mr. King yelled. "Do you have any idea how long it took to get through the cars! This is outrageous. I'm a very busy man and my time is very valuable. Why do you think I come here in the first place?"

"I'm very sorry, sir," said Lissa. "We're having a funeral here today, and it's our first one so things are a little cra-"

"That's not my problem," said Mr. King. "My time is valuable, and now you're just wasting more of it."

"Again, sir, I'm very-"

"Don't say sorry again," he snapped. "Now, give me a number six without all that stuff about place and plan."

Number six was a prayer for people in times of conflict. It was mostly made up from Psalms and involved a fair amount of asking God to do terrible things to the enemies of David. Stuff like sterility and drowning and even a horrible bit where they are melted like snails with salt. It wasn't a prayer that Lissa liked very much, and her only consolation was that it was rarely asked for. Most people stuck to the number two, which was all about learning to forgive your enemies and was much more in keeping with the times.

Woodlake's did try to soften the six with some bits about understanding how everyone has a place in God's plan and how those who deny Him shall suffer judgment only so that they may know Him, but Mr. King specifically asked her to drop those bits.

Usually rewriting on the fly was one of Lissa's unique talents, but today was anything but usual. Just as he had on her first shift, Mr. King began to constantly correct her on her wording, especially if she sanded over the wrath of the divine.

Halfway through her recitation he asked, "Are you Chinese?"

149

"I'm sorry, what?" said Lissa, confused.

"Are. You. Chinese?"

"I'm… well, I'm a quarter Chinese, yeah. My mom is half-Chinese, half-white, and my dad is all white. Why?"

"Well let me tell you something," said Mr. King. "I know a Chinese fella over in the next town that handles all my needs at the auto part store. He never makes a mistake. I thought that was all Chinese people, but I'm starting to assume that maybe you need someone to tell you that. I'm going to ask him if he'll come over here and help you be a better Chinese because clearly you're making them look bad."

"But… I'm more white than Chinese!" shouted Lissa, grasping at any piece of logic to throw back at this hateful man.

"No, you're not," said Mr. King. "I can tell by looking at you. I'm going to speak to your manager after you're done wasting busy people's time with this funeral."

He craned his head to look past Lissa into Nevaeh's coffin.

"She looks like a lesbian with that haircut, anyway," he said. "Probably died of AIDS. You should be more considerate of Christians than this."

And off he drove.

Dexter came up to Lissa, still standing in stunned silence. He took her shoulders and said, "Don't worry. It's okay. Let's just finish this, and we can go home."

In plane crashes, there is never a single cause. People in the industry call it the cascade of events. A faulty sensor gets replaced in a foreign airport that is a hub for black-market parts sold cheap. This particular plane fails the autopilot when the sensor gets a certain reading, and the failsafe backup was left off the checklist, thanks to an interrupted system update at the home airport. The pilot for this flight was an emergency replacement

only newly trained on this model because his alternative came down with an impressive strain of the flu. Tiny little mishap after tiny little mishap, each one not enough to cause a crash on its own, but as they build, they speed a plane to an unavoidable doom. All it takes is that one final fault and the whole thing comes down.

When Lissa heard Dexter repeat almost verbatim what she'd said to Nevaeh in their first awful meeting in this place, that was Lissa's final fault. She crashed, and her carefully built air of spiritual professionalism broke away, revealing the teenage girl in pain beneath.

She stumbled from Dexter's grip and walked with stiff legs behind the counter and out of sight from all that was going out. Up front, the Woodlake's crew was happy as clams in their attention. Lissa sank into the darkest corner she could find, and prayed her own prayers to be left alone. To not be found. She wanted to be in her car, away from this place. She wanted to be singing the songs she'd sung with her friends. She didn't want Alonso or Sheryl to tower over her and tell her how disappointed they were in a display like this. She was a deacon and a manager. She should be better than this. Maybe she wasn't up to the job after all.

Lissa put her hands over her ears to drown out the sounds of the world. She wasn't sure who she was even praying to anymore. She just wanted it all to go away. The voices and the loss and the sorrow and that screaming, piercing noise and her tears soaking through her clothes.

Wait, why was she all wet? She opened her eyes and saw the flashing lights of the fire alarm. The small, red boxes on the wall were producing a terrible shriek, and the sprinkler system had turned the small building into a hurricane. She slowly stood up and looked out into the main room. Reporters and employees and patrons were all fleeing through the doors to get away from the water. Outside it was starting to go dark, and in the far distance, Lissa heard fire trucks approaching. Was there a fire? What happened?

"Lissa."

She turned around, and there was Dexter. In his arms was cradled the body of Nevaeh. Dexter Lilley was never going to be a dashing figure, squat and mean and sure to one day be fat as his fleshiness testified. But there, in the pouring rain from the ceiling and the steel in his eyes, he was like an image of a saint to Lissa.

Nevaeh's head was thrown back over Dexter's arms, and as the drops hit her, it looked like she was crying. Well, now it was all three of them together.

"What are you doing?" asked Lissa.

"Something deeply illegal and metal as shit," he replied. "This place have a back door?"

Lissa nodded.

"Lead on," he said.

Through the drenched and quickly flooding back area of Woodlake's, Lissa led Dexter, who tenderly maneuvered Nevaeh through the cramped space. He was careful not to bump her head or

154

feet. Eventually, they came to the back door and Lissa led them out of the drenching water and outside.

"Open the back seat door," he said, gesturing to her car.

"I thought you were saving her body from the fire," said Lissa. "What's going on?"

"There isn't a fire," said Dexter. "I hit the alarm. We're going on a road trip. Please open the door. She's not as light as she looks."

Lissa hesitated for a second and then did as she was asked. She even squeezed in first to help guide Nevaeh gently into the back seat. As she feared, her friend's skin was indeed cold, but so was Lissa's after being soaked and thrown out into the December air. She looked around guiltily, but so far no one had come around the back to see them committing body theft. Christ, where was this going?

Eventually, they got Nevaeh propped up and leaning against the passenger side door with the seatbelt on her. Lissa crawled out of the back seat and started to walk to the driver's side. Dexter stopped her.

"I'll drive," he said. "I know where we're going."

"Where's that?"

"Galveston," said Dexter. "We're going to Galveston and do this the right way. No more of the Burger King of the Jews stuff. No more, you hear me? I didn't get to her in time to keep that bitch on her cell phone from hitting her, but I'm here now. You in?"

Lissa saw her perfect little life spiraling out of control. No, going off the rails. She'd jumped the track and now the inertia was going to decide where the train finally stopped. Without another word, she dropped her keys into Dexter's hands, and they got in the car.

Dexter had no trouble starting the Bug and getting it going, but he was unfamiliar with the dash controls. After a small bit of cursing, Lissa reached over and helped him crank the heat up so they could dry. Over the back of the passenger seat was her old blue jean jacket that had belonged to her grandfather. It was several sizes too large and perfect to wrap herself in.

Lissa buttoned the coat and pulled her arms inside. Decently covered, she unbuttoned her wet Woodlake's shirt and her bra. She fished them through the arm of the jacket. Underneath the voluminous coat, she was topless, but she was a now a good deal warmer for being dryer.

They passed more fire trucks as they headed south. Apparently no one had figured out what had happened yet. Waves of guilt began to wash over Lissa. They'd stolen a body, after all.

Or maybe they'd just stolen it back.

"Look," said Dexter. "It's going to be a long drive to the Gulf. Just to be absolutely completely honest about everything right now, I might have done a little meth earlier today. So, I'm awake and I know the way pretty much like the back of my hand from all those trips with Dad. Why don't you get some sleep, and you'll be awake by the time we get there?"

"Sleep? In the middle of a felony?" asked Lissa. "No, I'll stay up and keep you company."

156

"Suit yourself, Lissa," he said. And she did try very hard to suit herself. At first, she talked a bit about how she couldn't believe the people that she had seen at her job. When that started to seem petty with Nevaeh in the back seat, Lissa tried to speak about her, but everything felt muted and strange. Inquiries about what exactly they were doing were met with "You'll see" or grunts.

After an hour, Lissa was sitting in silence and indeed beginning to doze off. Every few minutes she'd start awake again, then settle back down with her head on her shoulder. From the right angle, she could see Nevaeh in the back seat in the rearview mirror. She looked peaceful.

It's "Heaven" backward, thought Lissa. Backward in the mirror. Her name is "Heaven" backward. Why did I never put that together before?

With that thought, Lissa's plane finally hit the ground and the world went black around her.

***

It was impossible for Lissa to put a name to the feeling at first because it was the first time she'd ever felt it. There were lips pressed against hers, soft and thin, and she felt a tongue that tasted of strawberries slide into her mouth and coax her own out in response. It felt like the first breath of life.

There was a weight on her chest, a delicious, warm weight that writhed and sought to touch her all down the length of her body. She felt breasts pressed against her own, and a tight belly whose bare navel dripped a sweet smelling sweat down onto her.

157

She felt two large hands on her shoulder blades in an embrace lift her into the kiss until not a single molecule of air could have passed between their lips. Propped against the door of her car, she pulled the buttons on her jacket and was rewarded with a warm hand sliding onto her bare breast. She gasped at the touch, feeling the lithe thumb of the hand pass over her nipple in terrible ecstasy.

Seeking a similar response, needing one, Lissa dove her left hand into the storm cloud hair she couldn't see with her eyes closed, but that she knew beyond a shadow of a doubt was there. Her hands, strong from the grips of a thousand desperate prayer sessions took a solid chunk of the girl's hair and drove her head back…

(Her head thrown back over Dexter's arm, the sprinklers dripping tears into her dead eyes. Her poor dead…)

And moved her mouth down to fasten on her swan-like neck. Braced against her tall frame, Lissa's right hand found itself sliding down between the legs of the girl. A gentle, but powerful squeeze rewarded her with her own name whispered and shouted at the same time. Her name…

(You're too stupid to even write your own name on the first try, let alone be the sort of person that can be a deacon. You're no good…)

Without opening her eyes or even being really aware how on Earth it was happening, Lissa knew that she and her were completely naked. Every inch of skin burned from the barest touch, and Lissa drowned in the feeling of wanting and being wanted. She understood now. She felt what it meant to feel. This was the fire you used to keep away the dark of an unfair and uncaring word. This was an old worship, a faith more ancient than Babylon or Egypt or Israel. For this angels would rebel and prophets would allow themselves to die on crosses.

Pressed down again by the girl, Lissa was afraid to name her. It would be like looking into the naked face of God. She trusted herself only to feel and taste and smell and hear.

"It's okay," said the girl. "Just a little more, and we can go home."

(Nevaeh's scared face in the dark. Lissa comforting her in the back seat when she was afraid of a cruel judgment. Their fingers weaved like chain mail…)

Lissa arched her back, and the girl moved down her body, planting kisses like she was sowing a harvest to be reaped later. Tentatively, Lissa's hand crossed over the girl's back. There she found something strange. Over the shoulders were thick ropes of scars that felt huge in the darkness. Her thoughts turned once again to the man from *The Scarlet Letter* who would whip himself to punish himself for lustful thoughts.

No, there was something else here. As she pressed her hands to the wounded back of the girl kissing her, Lissa felt the skin part and something bony and powerful begin to emerge from the shoulder blades. Briefly, she was afraid, but whatever pushed itself out from the girl soon turned from hard to soft. Between her fingers, Lissa struggled to find a name for what she was feeling. It came to her suddenly.

Feathers.

Nevaeh was growing wings.

***

Lissa was aware of a touch on her shoulder. It was Dexter, gently shaking her awake. They were parked on the deserted seawall of Galveston. In winter, there were not many people that braved the wind off the water in the morning, even for a brisk jog. The sun was rising reluctantly ahead of them.

Off to the right, a wooden pier stretched quite a distance into the Gulf of Mexico.

"We're here," said Dexter needlessly. Lissa nodded sleepily and got out of the car to stretch her legs. She looked briefly into the back seat, where Nevaeh was still dead. She looked peaceful. Asleep.

Sitting on the hood of the car, the two friends didn't say anything for a minute. Dexter handed Lissa a bottle of water and some travel cereal he had picked up from a gas station while she was dreaming. Lissa accepted both graciously. She had no idea how hungry and thirsty she was.

Hunger sated, Lissa finally asked what the plan was.

"Viking funeral, remember?" said Dexter. "That's how she wanted to go out, and I say we give it to her. I figure we lay her down at the end of the pier, wrapped in the blanket you have in your trunk, douse her at the end of the pier with gasoline and light it up. Eventually, it'll burn and collapse into the water. Good enough, I suppose."

"We're going to go to jail for this," said Lissa. "You know that, right? Even if we stop right now, we're going to be in the most serious trouble we've ever been in. Our whole lives could be ruined."

"Yeah," said Dexter. "But you know what? At least we got lives to ruin. And souls to save. I'm just tired of it, Lissa. Tired of seeing what I saw in Woodlake's. That's not salvation. I'm sure you did your best, but, well, faith is pain. You can't whitewash it and lay it over with linoleum. Faith needs blood. It's easy for all those people to talk about God and stuff when their biggest problems are whether or not their kid makes quarterback. My worry is, how do I live with myself knowing that I let them turn one of the few people I could ever be bothered to give a damn about into something to gawk at from a drive-thru window? That I let someone call that holy.

"Way I figure it, I can either get in trouble now when I might at least get forgiven and called young and romantic and some other horseshit. Or I can keep on walking their path and eventually I can put a bullet in my head. Or someone else's.

"So - you up for this or not? 'Cause I care about you enough to walk that path if you say no."

Lissa watched the sun come up and the cold night start to fall apart into mists and beams of light through the grey clouds. Dexter was right. Faith was a willingness to walk through a fire not because it would protect you, but because it would get you as far through it as possible, and maybe a little further still.

She hopped off the hood and looked at him. Then she nodded.

161

"Leave her in the car," she said.

Dexter looked at her puzzled, then quickly scooted off the hood as Lissa walked around and started the engine. Carefully, she drove down the length of the pier, praying that the old wood would hold. It was probably never designed to bear this sort of load, but despite the snaps, cracks, and protests from beneath her, it held. She stopped just inches from the edge and got out of the car. Opening the back door, she reached in to grab her Woodlake's shirt and bra. For a long moment, she stared at Nevaeh's body, remembering the dream of her touch.

Dexter jogged up and opened the trunk. Apparently he'd also acquired a can of gasoline and a lighter from the stop while she'd been asleep. Lissa began to wad up her shirt and try to feed it into the gas tank.

"No, no," said Dexter. "That's not right. Take the shirt, soak it in gas, and then leave it on top of the tire closest to the gas tank. That's the best way to make a car go up completely."

"How on Earth do you-"

"Do you really want to know why the son of a used car salesman has this information?"

Lissa didn't and followed Dexter's instructions exactly. Then they used the last of the gasoline on the car and the pier beneath it and left a small trail leading away. When they judged that they had enough distance, Dexter laid down the gas can and waited.

"You didn't get to say anything at the funeral," he remarked. "Are you going to say anything now?"

Lissa didn't know what to say, but something came to mind. In a tired, but clear voice she sang.

Will the circle be unbroken?

By and by, by and by.

Is a better how awaitin'?

In the sky. In the sky.

There are loved ones in the glory

Whose dear forms we've often missed

When you end your Earthly story

Will you join them in their bliss?

Woodlake's didn't allow singing, Lissa realized. She and other people had been reprimanded for it. All the music that was allowed was the recordings. Alonso told her it was because they were afraid of being sued for unauthorized use. Lissa realized that a church without song is not a church. She bent down to light the flames, and watched them race toward her beloved Beetle.

In the joyous days of childhood,

Oft they told of wondrous love,

Pointed to the dying Saviour;

Now they dwell with Him above.

You remember songs of Heaven

Which you sang with childish voice,

Do you love the hymns they taught you,

Or are songs of Earth your choice?

The fire had reached the shirt, and true to Dexter's word it was mere minutes before the car was beginning to shoot flame from every opening. Beneath it, the pier was beginning to buckle and crack as burning oil dripped like blood onto it, and the surface of the wood caught fire. The ominous groaning was beginning to grow louder, and behind them, voices were starting to shout as Galveston realized something was going on. Soon there would be sirens to drown her out, but Lissa kept on singing.

One by one their seats were emptied,

And one by one they went away;

Now the family is parted,

Will it be complete one day?

Will the circle be unbroken

By and by, by and by?

Is a better home awaiting

In the sky, in the sky?

With a crash, the pier collapsed under the heat and weight, and the Beetle tumbled out of sight. The waters quenched most of the fire. The frame bobbed briefly in the ocean, and then it was gone. With it went Nevaeh to her rest and Lissa felt finally free.

Dexter and Lissa turned around. There, at the end of the pier, were fire trucks and policemen. They were shouting at them, but neither teenager could make out what they were saying. With their hands up in the air, they walked toward the authorities to face whatever punishment was coming.

Dexter was handcuffed first, slammed face-down onto the hood of the police cruiser. The large man that held him asked him his name, and he gave it to them.

Lissa was allowed to remain standing, and they were gentle with her. God knows nobody wanted to have a video showing any brutality to such a tiny girl make the news. Lissa kept smiling, feeling freer in handcuffs than she'd felt in months.

"What's your name, ma'am," asked another large, gruff policeman.

"Niermann. Alice Niermann," she said, still smiling. "No, wait, sorry. It's not Alice.

"My name is Lissa."

Ceridwen's Cauldron

"Can you make it a little faster than last time?" said Lucas.

"Sure, sure," his wife nodded, grabbing up a wicker basket from the front of the store and heading in with a smile over her shoulder. "I promise we won't be long this time.'

"You always promise that," he muttered to himself. He turned and saw one of the tattooed, dark-haired sales girls looking at him with a knowing grin. Lucas returned it because she was pretty but still resented being eavesdropped on by a clerk. Resented being in this place at all.

Ceridwen's Cauldron was a chain of bath product counters that started springing up inside the big department stores around three years ago. It was very fancy stuff, all handmade and organic and cruelty-free and plenty of other stuff Lucas thought of as nonsense. It was all well and good to want to smell nice, but he didn't think of bathing as an event or an art. You get in, wash off the day's work, and then get on with your life.

It was also damned expensive, not that they couldn't afford it. Suveda had been out of law school for several years and was now effectively doubling their income from the chain of liquor stores that Lucas owned. They certainly had the money to drop ten bucks on a fizzy bath bomb that turned the water purple and smelled of lavender and primrose, but it seemed vaguely pretentious to do so.

Lucas Segura had grown up hard. His mom died when he was quite young, and his dad was not a warm man. Stuck with his only son in a bad part of town, he'd clawed and saved (and, Lucas was certain, stolen and sold drugs) until he was able to make an offer on a corner shop where the previous owner had a bad habit of drinking his stock. Any half-decent business man can make money selling vices in ghettos, especially when you've got your own stock boy you don't have to pay in the form of your offspring.

So Lucas grew up hauling heavy crates and watching people ruin themselves as his dad pocketed handfuls of cash. By the time he was eighteen, there were six stores and Lucas was managing half of them. When he was twenty-one, his dad turned over half his ownership and full control of the company to his son and promptly fled back to his birth country of Costa Rica to live well on his share. Lucas flew out every May to visit the old man and his new young wife and children, and Enrique Segura came to America alone every Thanksgiving.

All his life, Lucas had been told by white people that he was supposed to be fiery and hot-tempered. All Hispanics were. Lucas just shrugged. What did they know?

He watched Suveda wander among the bins, happily picking up everything that caught her eye and smelling it with a look of divine ecstasy on her face. The little corner of Nieman Marcus smelled wonderful, Lucas admitted, but there was something slightly addictive in his wife's movements. He was a keen spotter of chemical need in people. His livelihood depended on it.

"Would you like a demonstration, sir?"

Lucas turned and the girl from earlier was standing close to him and still smirking. At this distance, he noticed that she was older than he first supposed. Somewhere in her mid-forties. Clearly too old to be working in a place like this. A woman of that age should be fostering a real career or raising children, he thought. Either way, she was far too decorated for his tastes and raised his hackles despite the full curves highlighted by her tight, black clothing.

"I'm just waiting for my wife," he said politely enough, indicating Suveda as she talked excitedly with another clerk.

"Oh, you're Suveda's husband!" gushed the clerk. "She talks about you all the time. Just goes on and on about how wonderful you are. She'll probably be a while. She usually is. Sure I can't tempt you into trying something out?"

He looked at the woman, still holding onto his courtesy despite the fact he would much rather be left alone to wait for this whole thing to end. Her name tag declared her "Star." He gritted his teeth and reminded himself that people don't name themselves. She was just doing her job. No different from the former cheerleaders and pageant queens that set up in his stores and asked customers if they would enjoy trying a new kind of wine or whiskey. Eye candy to go with the mouth candy. Or skin candy, he guessed in this case.

What the hell. Might as well get something free out of this. It wouldn't make a dent in the dough Suveda dropped in here, but it was something. Maybe he'd even like it.

With a nod and a shrug, he allowed Star to lead him over to a small basin of water set on a tile of marble. The brown containers were filled with cream-colored ointments and spongy materials. Without asking, the woman unbuttoned his right cuff and began rolling up his sleeve. He bristled at the touch but said nothing as she dipped his hand and forearm into the basin to wet it before gently lifting it out.

"This is aloe mixed with rosewater," she said as she gently rubbed a crumbly substance into his skin. Her touch was gentle but slightly weird. He was reminded of the flesh of a stingray he had once petted at an aquarium touch tank. He grunted affirmation but did notice that the friction of her movements disappeared as she worked the stuff up and down his arm and between his fingers. It wasn't unpleasant.

Star rinsed his hand and arm some more in the basin, the water foaming and warm from the touch of the first product. Then she used a stick to dip into a bottle of cream and swirl it around in the bowl. Colors merged and formed in a whirlpool of hypnotic patterns. He was only barely aware of grunting a second affirmation when the clerk described what was in this one. Once again, his arm was in the water and Star's fingers danced around and up and down it.

Looking into the bowl, Lucas had a curious feeling. The water seemed completely transparent, yet also shrouded in mist at the same time. He could barely make out his own hand in it despite being only a few inches under the surface. There was also a strange heat. Not like burning, but... sunlight. That's what it felt like. His skin under the water felt like it was exposed to a warm summer sun. For a brief moment, he focused hard looking into the basin, and jumped slightly as he could have sworn he saw something large and alive pass by, like he had spied a whale from a porthole.

Pulling his arm out of the basin, Star dried it quickly with an expensive-looking cotton towel. Satisfied with her work, she guided his untreated hand onto the treated skin, and even Lucas had to admit it was a nice feeling. By contrast, the skin of his other arm looked rough and irritated, the lines on his hand deep and old. He frowned, somewhat offended his own skin should change that dramatically.

"Oh, what are you trying?" said Suveda, coming up to him with a kiss on the cheek. Star began to tell his wife of all the wonders of the product while Lucas shoved his

hands in his pockets and was pointedly distracted. Suveda insisted on buying what had been shown and her husband waited patiently while she was rung up.

It's her money, he thought. As they walked back through the store toward the exit, Lucas looked back, and Star gave him a cheery wave.

***

"See? It wasn't long," said Suveda as she maneuvered the big SUV through the narrow streets of downtown. The car had been his present to her when she passed the bar. It was a monster, a rare beast with a manual transmission in this day and age. Suveda loved the mass of it, and her grip on the stick shift was always white-knuckled and powerful. She treated it like she was whipping the car along the road. His wife's driving terrified Lucas despite her flawless driving record. He often hung onto the strap beside his window in a way that looked casual but was really him holding on for dear life.

"No," said Lucas. 'It wasn't."

"Did you like the Cosmic Cream she used on you?" she asked. "It sure felt nice to me."

"Yeah," he said. "It was alright, I guess."

Suveda looked at him. She was a fundamentally positive person who rarely wore a frown. Lucas recognized that she made a good counterweight from his usually grim, cold personality and was, in general, very grateful to have her energy directed through him. She was as tough as he was, though, and a frightening presence to her legal opponents. Sometimes Lucas wondered what she saw in him at all.

"It wouldn't kill you to pamper yourself a little sometimes," she said. "Part of happiness is recognizing that you are worth good things happening to."

"It's just soap, honey," he said.

"Sometimes," she replied. "Sometimes, it's just soap. Sometimes, it's a reward for a hard day. Sometimes, it's consolation for a bad day. Sometimes, it's an excuse to be by myself. And sometimes, it's bait for you to take me to bed with you."

"You don't need fancy soap for me to go to bed with you," he said in a somewhat condescending way. "You're beautiful, and I love you."

"I know I don't need it," she said in her lawyer voice. "But it's fun for me. I like to feel, hmmm, invested in. Yeah, that's the word. I invest in myself as something valuable. It's like detailing a car or putting a nice frame on a picture. You get me?"

"I guess," replied her husband.

***

It was Saturday afternoon, and Lucas was bored out of his mind.

He was bored most Saturdays. For thirty-nine out of the fifty-two weeks in a year, Suveda attended a local women's shelter's support group for the survivors of rape and sexual assault. She had missed only a handful of them in the five years they had been together, including for their wedding.

Suveda didn't like to talk about what happened to her when she was nineteen. At least, she didn't like to talk about it with him very much. He knew that a friend of her brother's had done something to her. She'd described it a little and Lucas didn't really think that what she was talking about was rape, exactly, not in a technical sense. It certainly didn't seem to be the sort of thing that someone should still be hung up on all these years later.

After all, he'd once been beaten so badly in school that he'd lost two teeth. Three boys had slammed his head into a metal trashcan and told him, "Happy to escort you home." Then, while he was busy trying to get the world to stop spinning, they'd dumped a load of trash and rotting food on him. "All tucked in for bed," one of them said. He'd never gotten those teeth fixed, but you could only see them if he smiled very big.

When Lucas asked Suveda if the guy was arrested for what he did, she'd shaken her head. As far as Lucas was concerned, if the asshole wasn't in jail, it just couldn't have been that bad. Her brother hadn't beaten the dude up or even stopped talking to him from what Lucas could gather. If he'd had a sister, he was sure he would have done something.

Whether he felt she was clinging to her victimhood or not, he admitted she was doing good work with the shelter, counseling and talking to survivors. Some of the stories she brought home were truly chilling. Father and grandfathers forcing little girls and even a few boys to do sick things for years of abuse. People married to monsters that humiliated them and broke them down. It was all Lucas could do to listen patiently as his wife poured out these experiences.

He tried to be supportive of her volunteer work and the people she ministered to. He thought the ones that left and came to his wife were very brave. He wished that others who didn't leave similar situations weren't too weak to do so.

Suveda used to invite some of her charges home for dinner but hadn't done so in the last year or two. Just as well; the conversations were always awkward.

So Lucas wandered around the house. There was nothing to clean or to repair. Nothing that needed his attention. He despised social media and had no real interest in playing around on the computer. The expensive video game console he'd been gifted with last Christmas hadn't been touched in a month. The shooting games that had come with it were fun enough, but he couldn't remember where he had stopped in the story and didn't want to start over. He'd endlessly re-read the few books he liked, and the thought of an unproductive day scrolling through TV made him feel useless. He was on the verge of taking a completely unnecessary shower when the house phone rang.

"Hello?" he said.

"Hi! Mr. Segura?"

"Yes," he said. "Who is calling, please?"

"This is Star, the manager at Ceridwen's Cauldron in the Galleria," said the voice. "I was calling for Suveda. Is she in?"

"No, Ms...."

"Star," she said with a giggle. "Just Star, Mr. Segura."

"Okay, Star," he replied with a sigh. "No, I'm afraid she's not in right now. She's at her-"

"Oh my Goddess!" said the manager. Lucas rolled his eyes at the evocation. "That's right. It's Saturday. I completely forgot what day it was. You ever do that?"

"I can't say that I have," said Lucas.

"She's totally at the shelter today," said Star. "That's so awesome that she does that for people. You must be extremely proud of her, especially considering her own experiences. I've been to her sessions myself, you know? She's so kind and caring."

"Yes, she is. I am very proud of her," said Lucas. Actually, what was going through his mind at the moment was how inappropriate it was that some tattooed pagan or whatever knew something so intimate about his wife. He couldn't imagine sharing something so personal with a member of his staff, and he'd probably fire anyone that asked such a question. He had half a mind to report this woman for intruding on Suveda's privacy.

"Was there something I could help you with, miss?" Lucas continued. "A message I could take?"

"Right, sorry," said the manager. "It's been crazy around here lately. I was calling to let her know that the summer products she'd ordered were in stock, and I've got them all boxed up and ready for her to pick up and take home. We're here until nine o'clock tonight if she wants to come by after. Or-"

"I'll get them now," said Lucas. As much as he didn't like the place, he wanted any excuse to get out of the empty house. And it would be a nice surprise for Suveda.

"Awesome!" she bubbled. "We'll see you soon."

***

An hour later, Lucas was smiling to himself. Not only had he picked up the large box of bath products, but also a nice bouquet of roses, chocolates, and a wine that Suveda was fond of. She'd be home soon, and he was happily arranging his purchases on the coffee table so that she'd see it as soon as she walked in the door. He'd considered ordering dinner and picking it up, but Suveda sometimes ate on the way home, and he wasn't sure what she would be in the mood for. Oh, well, they could always order a pizza or go back out or something. Regardless, he was reveling in his little project when the phone rang.

"Hey, babe," he said. "Everything okay?"

"Um, no," said Suveda quietly. "Not really. I mean, I'm fine, but…"

"But what? Is it the car? Were you in an accident or something?"

"Oh God, no!" she said. "I'm so sorry. No, of course, you'd think that. I forgot the time. No, I'm okay, the car's okay, but we had an incident here."

Lucas waited patiently for her to get her breath.

"One of the women staying here… well, her husband found out this is where she was. I think her mom told him. God knows why.

179

Anyway, he showed up just as the meeting was over, begging, crying, saying she had to come home. She refused, and he started yelling about going to his car and shooting himself with the gun he kept there. Next thing you know Kevin, you remember Kevin? That nice old retired cop who works security for us? Kevin's trying to escort him away, and the two started fighting. We'd been in lockdown for about half an hour. The cops got here in five minutes and picked the guy up, but Kevin's in the hospital with at least a concussion, and the woman, Cassandra, is just in a terrible state."

"Can I help?" he asked. "I can come up there, and I don't know, stand outside the door, I guess."

"No," said Suveda. "I don't think that would be a good idea. Everyone is a bit jumpy right now. The sheriff's office sent a couple of female deputies down to patrol the block. I'm going to stay here for a bit, though. Maybe another hour. I just wanted to let you know."

"Oh, okay," he said, trying to keep the sigh out of his voice. "Yeah, that's fine. Have you eaten? I could bring you something."

"We've got sandwiches, and I'll pick up something to munch on when I'm driving. Tell me there's alcohol in the house."

"Yep!" said Lucas proudly. "Bottle of January's Girl, and I went and picked up your bath bomb order. It's all laid out here for you."

"You're the best," she said. "That's exactly what I'm going to need tonight. Go ahead and eat. Play a game or something. I'll see you soon."

They exchanged "love yous" and hung up. Lucas felt his shoulders slump, and he looked over the presentation he'd made. It seemed like a waste, now. He certainly doubted she was going to react to anything with squeals of delight today. He knew he shouldn't be annoyed, but he was. He was also hungry and decided to go across the street to El Rio's.

It was a little-known fact that some of the best hamburgers in the world exist off the menu at taquerias. Mostly they were for kids who refused to eat other food, but the cooks put the exact same love and care into creating them. Lucas had started trying out burgers from the little restaurants and food trucks in his neighborhood as a child, and now, he was thoroughly addicted to them. At El Rio's, the meat was seasoned with the same spices as the tacos but seared on and blackened. The toppings were shredded and fresh, and the buns were often hand-baked. Granted, you were usually stuck with tortilla chips or rice as a side dish instead of fries, but it was a small price to pay.

He sat at the little counter bar and ordered a St. Arnold and his burger. The barman knew him well, since Lucas came in whenever Suveda was otherwise engaged. She liked the place just fine but tired of it quickly if they went too often. Lucas usually just sat there silently, listening to the sounds of the diners around him and idly playing on his phone. He and the barman occasionally talked shop, soccer, or zombie films, but it rarely went deeper than that.

Tonight, though, El Rio's was quiet. Lucas was one of only three customers there. Weird. It wasn't a popular spot, but he'd never seen it so dead on a Saturday night.

"Did I miss a Super Bowl or something?" he asked when his beer arrived. "This place is a graveyard."

"Nah, man," said the bartender. "There was some sort of water main break a few lights down. The whole street is cut off in that direction. I imagine it'll pick up later. My bank account hopes so, at least."

The two men shared an easy silence. There was no one to call the barman away, and Lucas waited patiently for his food while sipping his beer. Feeling a little bad for all his server's lost tips, he offered to buy the man a drink and watched as another frosty St. Arnold's was pulled from the ice. They clinked bottles and the barman said, "Cheers."

"So, what's the wife up to, today?" asked the barman. "That's usually why you come in, right?"

"Big domestic violence case at her firm that she's working on," Lucas lied. "Some asshole that raped his wife and then attacked her when she went to the cops. It goes to court tomorrow.'

"Whoa, wait, how did he rape his wife?" asked the barman.

"I… I don't know," said Lucas. "I didn't ask. The usual way you rape someone, I guess."

"No, man, I didn't mean like, how," said the barman. "I meant, how can you rape your wife? She's your wife. You can't rape your wife."

"I'm not sure I'm following you."

The barman looked down at his beer for a moment and then took a sip.

"She shouldn't say no, you know?" he said. "That's what I mean. You get married, and like, sex is guaranteed. That's one of the upsides of the old ball and chain, am I right?"

Lucas thought about it. Suveda had only said no a handful of times in the years they'd been together. It was usually during her time of the month or simply because she was tired. There hadn't been a lot of sex in the house during her last semester of law school, that was for sure, but Lucas didn't feel angry at her for refusing out of exhaustion. He'd turned her down a few times during the holidays himself every year when things got crazy in the stores, and she never took it personally either.

"Well, I mean there have been times when she says she's tired, or you know, sick, or something."

"Oh yeah, man, I get you," said the barman. "That'd just be wrong to make a sick girl do it. That's not nice. But I mean, if she's not sick or anything, if she just doesn't want to do it, and you like, really need to do it, one of those situations, then yeah, for the marriage she should just go along with it, you know? She'll probably even get in the mood once it's going on. I bet your honey's case was something like that. The chick just doesn't understand what a marriage means, probably. I bet her dad wasn't around or something."

With that, the man finished his beer and went over to the other two occupied tables to see if there was anything that he could get them. The cook brought Lucas's burger out, and he asked if he could have it in a to-go container. He pretended to answer a text on his phone while it was bagged up and waved to the barman as he left the restaurant with his beer half-finished. What the hell, he had beer at home.

Walking back to the condo, Lucas thought about what the barman said. It confused him. Yes, a married couple should reasonably expect sex from each other at regular intervals, but was there a line that got crossed? The people that Suveda counseled sure seemed to think so, but they were almost all women. No one ever seemed to get the other side of the story. There's always another side.

Just as he reached the front door, Suveda drove up with a cheery double beep of the car horn. Lucas walked over to her with a big smile on his face, holding up the take-out bag from El Rio's as an answer to where he'd been. Rolling down the window, his wife laughed and held up a bag from the chicken sandwich place next door. She must have literally been in the drive-thru while he was talking in the bar.

The couple walked in the front door and discovered Lucas's neat arrangement had been largely demolished by their cat, Demon, an old, one-eyed Himalayan who had decided to wreak havoc in the name of trying to get into the chocolate box. Clawing through the cellophane appeared to have been too much for the animal, and he lay sprawled on the table in a tired heap, with the pleasant smelling carnage around him. Lucas was incensed, but Suveda found it amusing. She picked up the cat and, with the other arm hugged, Lucas for being so thoughtful. Then she made him kiss the top of the cat's head, which Lucas did before taking him and locking him in the laundry room so they could eat their take-out in peace.

After wine, fast food, slightly crushed chocolate, and a short recounting of the events at the shelter, Suveda took her box from Ceridwen's Cauldron to organize it in the linen closet, setting aside the stuff she'd picked out for Lucas in a small, separate bag, and announced she was going to take a bath. Once the water was running, her husband decided to maybe play a video game after all.

He let Demon out of the laundry room, and the cat curiously sniffed the table until it begrudgingly admitted there was no more food to eat. With a cold anger, it settled on the back of the couch to glare at him while Lucas fired up the system, deciding to start from the beginning of the game and hopefully stay more focused this time around.

It was about some sort of assassin, he remembered that pretty well. The guy was genetically altered to be a perfect, cold-blooded killer, but he turned on his masters and was now trying to save a little girl. That felt pretty good, thought Lucas. He would pick off guys in black outfits with a silenced pistol trying to get the girl to safety. It was hard, but he starting to get the hang of it.

When Suveda came out in her towel, Lucas was in some level where he had to hunt a target through a strip club. Dancers grinded on the stage with their bare breasts hanging out, and the sleazy pimp he needed to eliminate was holed up in a back room where three exotic-looking girls with broken English were giving him lap dances.

"Oh, you're playing your Christmas present," she said, kissing his cheek.

"Yeah," he replied. "It's better than I thought it was at first. Just needed to give it another shot, apparently."

"What's with the strippers?" Suveda asked.

"I'm trying to get to this human trafficking guy," he said. "I'm not sure what to do. I think I'm supposed to take this dead hooker's body in the back alley and leave it so the cops find it and raid the joint, and I then take out the guy in the confusion."

"You just pick up some corpse as part of the game?"

"I guess," he said. "I could also just start shooting and hide while it clears out, then go in. It's kind of weird. But fun."

Suveda told him to enjoy; she was going to bed. He paused the game long enough to give her a kiss and a slight squeeze on her bottom. She smiled against his lips and took Demon with her into the bedroom. Lucas went back to the game. Eventually, he had to use the dead hooker as bait after all, her frighteningly realistic nude body both erotic and horrifying as it sat under a street light staring up into the digital sky.

In the resulting mess, he got his assassin into the back room, but he missed his shot and accidentally put a bullet in the chest of one of the screaming girls. The other two ran, and his target ended up taking the second bullet in the back. A prompt jumped up congratulating him on the kill, and his tally score suffered a half a star penalty for the accidental murder of the stripper. It seemed kind of low, honestly, but what did he care. None of it was real, anyway.

***

It was Friday, a week later, and the two were in the bedroom getting the final odds and ends packed for a trip Suveda was making to her firm's central office. She was part of a presentation of yearly case statistics, her first year to be included. Both of them recognized that it was a big step on the path to partnership and better things, but Suveda was nervous. Opponents she could handle, but public speaking to her superiors often got her a little frazzled. Lucas imaged she would have more than one drink on the plane to calm down.

She was walking back and forth now, reciting her itinerary to herself over and over again, along with sudden realizations of things she needed to do. It was a little irritating, but Lucas was happy to help with the fetching of items, the checking of the weather in Chicago, and the confirmation of plane tickets and needed materials.

Finally, when it was clear there was no more preparation left to do, and there was still a half an hour before they needed to leave for the airport, she sat down on the bed and rubbed her temples.

"It's going to be okay, Suveda," said Lucas, tenderly rubbing between her shoulder blades.

"That feels nice," she said, leaning into his hand.

Lucas continued rubbing, enjoying the smooth skin. There was at least some benefit to all that goo she bought. She always felt amazing to touch. He started having some idea on how they could

187

spend that half an hour before she'd be physically absent for the next few days.

He leaned in and kissed her cheek while continuing to massage her. Then he moved his mouth down her long neck to leave butterfly kisses along the sensitive places. Suveda giggled at his tickling touch but stopped his other hand when it reached to cup her breast.

"We'd better not," she said. "I'm meeting corporate right off the plane, and I'm already going to be rumpled by travel. I don't think it would do to have mussed up hair and make-up from sex on top of that. Sorry, Luke."

Lucas continued kissing her neck and reached up his hand again to her other breast. He felt her nipple harden even as she started to swat his hand away. That was a sign of encouragement to him.

"You're not going to be here for days," he said, his mouth muffled against her. "C'mon, you know you're going to be lonely without me."

Gently, but strongly, he pulled her down with him even as she started to try and stand up. He turned her face toward him and kissed her, sliding his tongue into her mouth as she again started to protest and smearing her lipstick.

"Luke, baby, c'mon," she said as soon as she could. "I'm already nervous, and I don't have time for this right now. We'll do it when I get home, okay?"

He didn't even bother answering her this time, just rolled over onto her and pressed his strained erection against her slacks. His need for release was a pounding drumbeat in his head, and his hands started to work their way onto the snaps and zippers of her clothing. He wanted to feel her naked body against his. He wanted her to squeal his name when she came. It would be great.

He sat up briefly and looked down at his wife, decidedly more disheveled and flushed than she was a few moments ago. Her breathing was heavy and her eyes wide. He noticed the flush in her cheeks and the seductive way her clothes now hung from her after his pawing. Satisfied that he'd convinced her that this was a good thing, he smiled.

"I don't know why you were playing so hard to get," he said and dramatically pulled his t-shirt over his head.

The next thing Lucas knew, there was a sharp pain on the left side of his head, and he was seeing stars. Literally seeing stars that flashed in and out of his visions and he crumpled over and rolled off the bed with a meaty thud. He had just enough time to mentally remark that he finally understood why cartoon characters had a halo of stars around their heads after having an anvil dropped on them before he realized Suveda had brained him with their old alarm clock. It lay right beside him on the floor on his side of the bed, blinking 12:00 over and over again. Slowly, he got to his feet, feeling very woozy.

"What the fuck was that all about?!" he yelled. "That fucking hurt, honey. Am I bleeding?" He touched his head, looking for a cut.

"I'm sorry," said Suveda. Lucas looked at her and was a little frightened. Tears were pouring out of her eyes so fast, he could actually see the mascara running like a black waterfall. Her hands were gripped so tight in fists her olive skin was pale as snow at the knuckles, and he wondered if she'd cut herself with her nails. She looked like an animal in a trap, and he certainly wasn't going to risk having another piece of electronics aimed at him by approaching her.

Suveda bolted for their bathroom and locked the door behind her. Lucas heard her loudly sobbing as she yelled how sorry she was over and over and over again. Her husband gently knocked and tried for several minutes to coax her out of the room with sweet words and apologies. Eventually, Lucas settled for replacing the clock, resetting the time, making the bed, and going to sit in the living room to wait for her. He had no idea what else to do.

In the guest bathroom, he inspected his head. There was no break in the skin, but he was already sporting an impressive knot near the hairline. He splashed water on his face and fidgeted like he had as a child when his dad had caught him smoking.

About three minutes before they had to leave, he heard the bathroom door unlock and open. Suveda came out to the living room, make-up reapplied and in a different suit. Lucas stood up quietly, looking at her and having no idea what to say. He wasn't even sure what it was he'd done wrong.

"We, um, we need to go now," was all he could think to say. "You'll miss your flight."

"Okay," said his wife. Lucas walked past her to the bedroom to fetch her suitcase and wheeled it to the car. He stowed it in the back of the SUV and took his place in the passenger seat, buckling himself in. Suveda climbed up herself and started the car. The twenty-mile drive was laid out before them in what Lucas now considered a conversational minefield.

It was five minutes of silence before Suveda spoke, and it was in a strange, mechanical voice he'd never heard before.

"I'm very sorry that I hit you with the clock," she said. "I shouldn't have done that. I should have just said 'no' more emphatically. I don't think you understood what was going on."

"I still don't," said her husband. "I just thought, you know, plane rides always scare you and so do meetings like this. I figured you could let off a little steam. I didn't mean to-"

"I know you didn't mean anything by it," she said, her voice still flat and monotone like an automated menu reciting account information back at him. "I love you, Luke. I really do, but you can't do things like that. When you said I was playing hard to get, it was the same thing that... that he said when he... you know, to me, and I sort of snapped. It triggered something very bad, and I lost control."

"Sweetie," he said. "I'm not him. He's never going to hurt you again. I'm never going to do anything you don't want me to do."

"He is still hurting me," she said quietly. "He made me scared of my husband. He got me to hit you with a heavy object. He sent me crying into a bathroom almost a decade later."

Lucas said he was sorry, and Suveda nodded. He said he loved her, and she responded in kind. The rest of the trip happened quietly. When they arrived at the airport, Suveda got out, and Lucas got her suitcase for her. They embraced, kissed, and she promised to call him when she landed. Lucas got into the big, unwieldy car and left to return to his empty home.

***

Lucas was sitting alone at his dining room table, eating a reheated chicken dinner, when the house phone rang. Hoping it was Suveda, he picked it up on the second ring.

"Hello?" he asked.

"Hey there, again, Mr. Segura!"

"Oh, it's… Star, right?" he asked, disappointed.

"That's me! Often imitated, never done right," she responded cheekily. "Do you have a moment?"

"I suppose I do," he said. He really had no desire to talk with this weirdo, but he knew she was something like friends with his wife and wanted to be careful about anything that might upset her for a bit.

"I'm calling about an order Suveda placed this afternoon," she said.

"You must be confused, Star," he said. "Suveda's in Chicago on business for the next three days. She would have only just landed around 3 p.m. our time."

"Oh yeah, she said she'd just landed," replied Star. "She called me on my cell while I was at my writing group and asked if I could put together a package of something. It was pretty unusual stuff, I have to tell you. I had to drive to three different counters just to fill it up!"

192

Lucas was deeply angered and hurt. He'd been waiting for hours for a call from Suveda only to find out she'd apparently only bothered to inform a damned shop clerk that she'd landed safely. And for what? Another stupid box of bath bombs and soap that she couldn't even use until she got home on Tuesday. What kind of petty revenge was this?

"I'm sorry for your troubles in getting what Suveda wanted," he said through gritted teeth. "Especially considering that she's not due back for several days and has no use of them until then. It seems my wife has wasted your day off. I'll be sure to speak with her."

The laughter that came from the phone was loud and wild and strange. Lucas actually held the phone away from his ear.

"'Speak with her'," said Star. "That was good, Mr. Segura. You sounded just like one of the 50s TV dads or something when you did that. I totally pictured you with a martini and all in black and white just now. Suveda's right, you're hilarious."

Lucas was furious. Not only was Suveda apparently divulging aspects of their personal life with some silly shop girl, she was apparently mocking him to her as well. Star had a funny picture of him in her head? Well, now Lucas had a decidedly less funny one in his. He saw his wife and the trampy manager giggling at him over a bubbling sink as they rubbed their stupid soaps onto each other. He even briefly wondered if there was some sort of sick sexual relationship between the two of them since apparently she was worth a phone call and her own husband wasn't. The blood in his ears pounded with his anger, but Star chimed in before he could explode.

193

"Anyway, none of this is for her, so it's not a waste at all," she said.

"If it's not for her, then why exactly are you calling me in the middle of dinner?" he asked.

"Because it's for you," she said, and though smiles make no noise, Lucas could hear the one on her face. "Suveda said that you needed something, and asked if I could help her out. And I was happy to, of course, because she's so awesome and kind and giving. What's a day off for, if not to get something besides work done, am I right?"

Almost against his will, Lucas replied that he felt that way, too. What was going on?

"It's all ready, now," said Star. "Like I said, it's a bit unusual and special. You have to do it all in a certain order to get the desired effect. When would be a good time for me to come by?"

"Come by?" asked Lucas baffled.

"Uh-huh," chirped the woman. "You guys live over in Spring Branch, right? I'm actually just around the corner right now. Why don't you give me your address, and then finish your dinner? I'll be right over. Oh, wait, never mind. I have it in my store phone from the orders. See you in ten minutes."

With a click, she hung up, and Lucas stared at his phone. Five minutes ago, he was wondering if Star was sleeping with Suveda, and now she was on her way to… what? Give him a bath? This was creepy, and the second she was in the door, Lucas intended to get this all straight. No more wondering around in the dark waiting for answers and no more games where he didn't know the rules. This woman was going to know her place, and when Suveda got back, she'd better have some good answers.

***

Star knocked with "Shave and a Haircut" because of course she did. Lucas sighed and opened the door. She peeked her head around the side of the large paper sack and said, "Hi!"

Lucas decided to be chivalrous, at least, and take the bag from her. She did say she'd driven all over town getting the stuff after all, and he was surprised to find it much heavier than expected. He gently set the products on the living room table and turned to begin the talk that definitely needed to happen.

Star leaned against the closed front door with a bemused grin on her face. She was still in black despite being out of her work clothes, but her outfit was far more casual. Her large breasts pulled her tank top tight so it was slightly transparent, and the long skirt she wore was trimmed at the bottom with tiny bells. She wasn't wearing any shoes, and Lucas saw that she had a small frog tattooed on the top of her foot. Her tousled black hair was shot through with both purple highlights and the occasional strand of grey, held back with a headband that left her face open and free. Her eyes were calm as she looked at Lucas.

Suddenly, he didn't know what to say. The utter weirdness of the situation unmanned him. He wasn't even sure what he wanted to talk about anymore. Suveda hadn't called and didn't answer her phone when he tried her. She'd sent over this woman instead, and all this seemed like it was perfectly normal to everyone that wasn't him.

Lucas asked Star to sit, and she did so in the chair across from the couch where his wife often sat and read. Demon promptly hopped into her lap and settled immediately on her leg while glaring at Lucas. Idly, Star's hand ruffled the fur on his head.

"Your house is nice," said Star, completely relaxed and apparently at home. "You always wonder about people's houses when you just see them out and about in the world, don't you just? Everybody you meet has a little nest that perfectly reflects who they really are, just waiting for them when they're done talking to you. A safe place. Well, it's supposed to be, anyway."

Lucas wondered if Suveda had told Star about what happened with the alarm clock and if this was all some kind of weird metaphorical therapy.

"All your stuff is right angles," said Star. Lucas looked around. "It is?"

"Yeah," said Star. "All your picture frames match the height of your doors and then make ninety-degree turns down to define other lines in the room. If you took one of those laser leveler things and held it against every flat line on every wall, it would probably always match up with another somewhere else in the room. Some people do it consciously. Some people do it unconsciously. I think it looks like cage bars to me, personally, but if you're into modernism it's cool."

"I've never noticed before," said Lucas. "I'm very confused by all of this, miss. I don't know why you're here, really, and I don't understand hardly anything you say. My house is nice, but it looks like a cage. My wife doesn't call me when she lands but sends you over here with something I have no use of. Is this some kind of joke? Because it's not funny."

"Cages can keep things out just like they can keep things in," said Star. "It's all a matter of perspective. Are you ready, now? It's been a long day, and I'd like to get this over with."

The sudden hardness to her voice was startling. The shop girl was nothing but bubbly and bright and happy to help. She was like a scullery maid out of some BBC drama, except now she wasn't smiling anymore. Demon fidgeted on her lap until he leaped off her with a yowl. He looked back at her through his one eye then squeezed beneath the sofa.

The woman stood, the bells of her skirt jingling. Without a word, she picked up the sack she had brought and walked out of the living room to the master bathroom. It no longer even surprised Lucas she seemed to know the way.

He sat, strangely afraid. From two rooms away, he heard noises of things being put away and of water in the bathtub running. It was a sound he associated with Suveda, hopping into the tub after a long day. Smells began to flow out into the air. There were easy ones to identify like lavender and sage and sea salt, but there were others that didn't trigger any image at all. Lucas suddenly wanted to run out of his own house into the street with no reason why he should.

197

"Mr. Segura," came a whisper near his ear, and he jumped to his feet. Behind him, Star stood with her hands at her side. She had removed her top, and in addition to the tattoos of fairies and manticores and other strange things that decorated her torso, she had painted red circles around her large-nippled breasts and her stomach. These were accented with other angry red stripes, each designed to highlight her womanly curves. Her face was masked with a thick white paste that left her eyes in dark shadow. With languid ease, she gestured past her into the bedroom.

Lucas got up and silently obeyed, afraid not to. He skirted by her as far as the door frame would allow, and padded into the dark bedroom. From the master bath was a yellow glow. Candles sat on the flat surfaces, homemade smoky ones that seemed to use up all the oxygen in the room. He wondered how on Earth she could have had so many in the sack she was carrying until he light-headedly realized it was partly an illusion brought about by the two large mirrors.

He walked to the bathtub, conscious of the sound of Star's breathing behind him. The tub was full and boiling with a strange purplish froth. Or maybe it was crimson like good wine. It was hard to tell in the low light. The stream of water from the faucet seemed to be blasting out at a fantastic rate, far harder than he'd ever noticed it doing so before. It should have been filling the tub to overflowing, but the level never rose above a few inches below the edge.

He looked back at Star and her unreadable painted face, and he stepped aside as she motioned him from in front of her. Out of the sack on the floor, she drew out something nearly indescribable. It was crystalline and sinuous, like the tentacle of a giant squid that had been frozen, but not completely solid. From tiny cracks grew small pink flowers somewhere between a Morning Glory and a Lily. In Star's hand, the blooms seemed to drink in the air and exhale it, and the vaguely phallic branch exuded a combination of bizarre scents. Burning sand, candied blood, a pitcher plant full of rain, berries, dead insects, diet soda, and semen. Lucas reached to steady himself on the edge of the sink as he watched Star spit on the object, which hissed and steamed like her saliva was acid. With reverence, she laid it in the water, and colored bubbles floated up into the air in response.

Lucas Segura was not a religious man by any means. He rarely went to church outside of weddings and funerals, and the only Bible in his home had belonged to his mother and was kept purely for its sentimental value. He read its highlighted passages left by her hand on the anniversary of her death, but he never talked to God. Nonetheless, the word "abomination" was lighting up in his mind, screaming like a siren. His home had been transformed into something unholy and strange, and in his fear, he now understood why so many followers of new gods hunted and killed followers of old gods over the millennia.

Star wiped her hands on her skirt and turned to him. She placed her hands on his shoulders and pushed him down onto the toilet. Kneeling, she removed his shoes and socks, before standing him up and unbuttoning his shirt. The kiss of her fingers was electric. Lucas was certain that despite the fact that he was literally trembling in fear at the moment, when she reached his pants, Star was going to find him painfully erect. He hoped to whatever gods were listening it wouldn't offend her.

Once she'd shed all of his clothes, Star stood and waited, her face unreadable. Lucas opened his mouth to ask what he was supposed to do, then shut it without a word, sensing that he was supposed to know. On the one hand, he was naked with a topless woman in a bathroom lit with candles. It was a situation she had initiated, apparently with the full blessing of his wife. Was he supposed to kiss her? Were they going to get in the tub together? The smoke and heavy scents and the roar of the water made it hard to think. His cock certainly wasn't confused about what it wanted to do, but his brain was sure a misstep this time would cost him more than a sore head.

Hesitantly, he inched over to the tub. As he passed Star, his erection brushed against her thigh, but if it bothered her, she made no sign. Gingerly, he lifted his foot and placed it in the water.

The water felt like it was boiling hot, and whatever Star had added to it attacked his feet like those small fish that are supposed to eat the dead skin off people with psoriasis. With a yelp, he pulled his foot back out, but it looked totally normal. The lumps and boils were just the additives in the water flowing off his skin, nothing more.

With a sudden flash and what sounded like a suppressed impatient sigh, Star shot her arm out and gripped his member with brutal strength at the root. The move was anything but sexual, and

Lucas openly groaned from the painful pressure. Using his cock like a handle, she forced him to step over the edge into the tub, and then onto his back. Only when he was submerged to his neck did she relinquish her hold. Once again, she wiped her hands on her skirt, though with a slight appearance of disgust this time.

The water felt full, like a peat bog or quicksand. Things bubbled and crashed against his skin. The heat immediately caused him to start sweating, and there was a motion in the water that felt tidal. Still, new water gushed into the tub with no sign of stopping. He felt like he was melting in places, and the thought came to him that he would see chunks of his own flesh and bone bob to the surface any minute now. He cast his eyes up to the ceiling and saw that Star had used the same glowing white paint on her face to trace a moon cycle above him. At his feet, a new moon was a sliver in the dark, while above him was a full white circle.

Lucas suddenly realized he couldn't move. His limbs would not obey him. Only his eyes seemed capable of motion, and they frantically glanced left as a terrifying sound rang out.

Squatting on her heels, Star had removed an ornate dagger from the sack and pulled it from its sheath with a ringing, metal scream. Lucas remembered the harsh way she had handled him earlier and frantically tried to lift his arms, his legs, anything to get away from whatever she planned to do with the blade. If Star saw this, she gave no sign.

From one of the cheerily decorated containers from her store, she dipped out a blue fluid and proceeded to rub it up and down the length of the knife. It looked wicked sharp, but she somehow managed to keep from cutting herself. She set the container on the edge of the tub as she fished another from her seemingly bottomless bag. Lucas's eyes could make out the word "satori" on the label.

Her knife now anointed, Star stood and came to Lucas. She looked down at him for a moment before setting her foot on the edge of the tub. The small green frog tattoo seemed alive on her skin, breathing in and out as it watched him like a fly. Lucas internally thrashed, trying to will his arms to grab her ankle and trip her, make her knock her head out on the floor, but he could barely even wiggle.

With a slight grunt of effort, Star stepped her other foot onto the edge, bracing herself lightly with the shower rod. Her skirt blocked his view, but Lucas heard a solid thud above him. With a light hop, Star got down once more.

In the ceiling, the dagger was stuck right into the middle of the full moon, leaving an ugly, ragged gash in the plaster. Lucas glanced to Star, standing calmly beside him and then looked up again as he felt something hit his forehead.

It was blood. Big, fat drops of blood from the stabbed moon were running down the hilt of the dagger and landing squarely on his face with perfect rhythm. Tap. Tap tap. Tap. Tap tap.

It was aggravating beyond all measure. More than to escape, more than to understand what was going on, Lucas just wanted to get out from under the leaking knife. He wanted to wipe the blood, or whatever it was, off his face. Then he realized something truly frightening.

Each drop of blood was pushing him further down into the water. Millimeter by millimeter, he could feel himself sinking. He tried to brace himself with his feet, but it didn't even feel like they were there anymore. Within seconds, the water was over his chin and edging toward his mouth.

Lucas looked up at Star, eyes wide and terrified. He couldn't open his mouth to plead. Even if he could move the muscles, it would just send water down his throat. He tried to beg her with his eyes to save him, and she must have realized it because she started to laugh a low, throaty laugh.

The water was over his nose now. He held his breath, but already, his lungs were on fire, demanding new air. Two more drops, maybe three, and his eyes would be underwater. He blinked furiously to the shop girl to stop this.

Still laughing that odd, earthy laugh, which sounded enormous in his submerged ears, Star reached down and cupped Lucas under the chin. With easy strength, she lifted him slightly, and as his nose broke the water, he drew in a huge breath. Star held him that way for a second more and then shoved him as hard as she could down below the surface. Lucas managed to break his paralysis just enough to let out a silent scream, and the water entered him.

***

Lucas Segura felt himself sinking and tumbling in freefall, which was absurd because even if he was being drowned by some strange murderous witch, he was still in the bathtub, and it was only a couple of feet deep. His mind must be dying, he thought.

Hallucinating. In one last act of bravery, he decided to open his eyes and at least prove that he was being murdered normally.

All below him was a vast underwater landscape. A sunken city blazing with light twinkled as he dropped toward it like he was made of dense metal. There were strange eels in the water around him that bared their teeth and darted away as he invaded their territory. He spun and tried to look up above him, but there was nothing except the blackness of the ocean's surface far away.

Thankfully, he didn't seem to be drowning, but the sheer insanity of his surroundings led him to scream into the water.

From behind him, a dark shape zoomed by, and he tried to catch sight of it in the dark water. It was fast and always seemed just out of his peripheral vision until he felt sharp talons slam into his back and flippered legs wrap around his thighs. One hand gripped him by the forehead and arched him back until he was staring into a horrid face.

It was Star but not her. This Star was the color of a sand shark and clearly not human. No one feature reminded him of the strange shop girl, but all put together, she couldn't be anyone else. Her eyes glowed in the water.

With a flick of an unseen tail, Star drove Lucas further and further down, turning his head to look at the city below as they approached at an alarming speed. It was beautiful, but Lucas was sure he was going to die there.

He felt a lipless mouth and small dagger teeth near his ear.

"In sunken Guyth, there is a ceremony that has been performed for hundreds of years," she hissed sweetly. "The Vails, the temple prostitutes that head their most powerful church, send their most holy and skilled priestesses to pray and lie with the king on this day each year. Or queen. Or both. The Vails themselves started it when Guyth was young, and the exiled rightful heir was sheltered in their temples as he hid from his murderous aunt. Once he reclaimed his throne, he thanked the Vails for their kindness by legitimizing their religion and extending protections to them from abuse and thieves in addition to converting to the faith formally himself.

"The high priestess blessed the king herself in thanks, and the Vails have blessed every ruler since on the anniversary. It was a beautiful and holy thing, with the selection of the annual willing participant a source of great speculation and a commentary on the guidance that the realm was needing to receive. During a persecution of the Inns race, the king was sent a member of that people every year for three years until he reformed the laws and ended the oppression. A blind girl ministered to a narcissistic vainglorious king who squandered the treasury on icons of himself. A former soldier who had overcome many massacres and lost many friends was dispatched to a queen sick with despair after her sister had been killed on a diplomatic mission waylaid by a rebel group. The Vails are called the Pathmaidens, renowned for their guidance of the regent.

"But the current king ascended the throne young. He was cruel then, and decades later, he is crueler still. For the first several years, the Vails blessed him with young girls of incredible beauty and immeasurable kindness. These returned to the temple bleeding, hurt and badly used. When the next year came, the high priestess herself went to the king, and though she was too powerful to refuse, he ended the ritual as quickly as possible and spread malicious poison to the court about how uncomely and unskilled she was in the bedchamber. For several years afterward, the king did the unthinkable and came to the temple to select his blessing personally, and fearing further injured members of the church, the Vails complied as he eroded their power and mocked their faith.

"Finally, in desperate protest, the Vails sent him a five-year-old girl in their care, a happy child who would one day train to serve the church. She was selected because she was the same age as the king's own daughter and much resembled her in manner. The high priestess hoped that the king would see the girl not as a Vail but as a child. That he would refuse to lie with her and instead hear her prayers and see the cruelties he inflicted both on the church and on all his people.

"That hope was in vain. The king took the child as a woman and then had her killed by his guards. He blamed the rape and murder of the girl on her escort, who was put to a slow torture and death. He called the high priestess a monster for employing such a man and

207

called for her arrest. She committed suicide before it could happen. The power of the Vails was ended.

"Since then, the former members have taken their temple wealth and hidden from the king under the guise of a company that seeks to extract energy from the core of the planet. He funds them lavishly, using the promise of free power as bait to keep his ever-more battered subjects willing to endure his abuses. What he doesn't know is that the Vails are in reality aiming to open the core to the sea in order to crack open the planet itself."

Lucas listened to the tale in rapt attention as the city he presumed was Guyth grew larger in his vision. Once it was obscured by a massive, tentacled beast passing by, but nothing could blot out the vast metropolis for long. The story Star gleefully whispered in his ears was horrifying and cruel. It couldn't possibly be true.

"Tonight on the holy night, the last of the Vail high priestesses is seeking an audience with the king for one final chance at salvation. She's dressed in the finest clothing left to the order and wearing jewels that are older than recorded history. She is speaking right now in the banquet hall. Now she is being seized. They're stripping her and her gown is ripped. She's held on a table, feeling food underneath her backside and cutlery against her shoulders. She prays, but she does not beg. The king doesn't even bother to disrobe, simply fishing himself out of his clothes and messily climbing on top of her.

"Even when he shoves himself inside her, she holds back. She's still praying. Still trying to be the Pathmaiden. Her words are annoying the king, and he orders one of his nobles to put his hand over her mouth while he finishes. Even as he's done and she can feel his seed dripping from her, she still tries. It's only when the king walks away and callously calls for another to mount her that she says a final prayer to her goddess and bites down on the remote control in her hollow tooth starting the final drilling."

Below him, there was a sound in the sea that has never been heard before and will never be heard again. It was the sound of an ocean falling into a fire of molten rock. The fire turned to stone and liquid to air at a rate of millions of transactions a second. Pillars of light shot screaming up on all sides of him as the sheer force sent white hot balls of nickel and iron the size of skyscrapers heavenward as if Hell itself was launching an attack.

Lucas could see people running out of the buildings below, desperately trying to swim away as fire engulfed them and explosions tore them apart. In the spire-like keep in the middle of the city, the walls turned to slag and then cooled a second later into a twisted mockery of the original architecture.

With a screeching laugh, Star released her clawed grip from his skin, and Lucas felt a hard kick in his back. He sank at high velocity into the approaching inferno where water was stone and air was fire. His skin blistered, and his eyes stopped seeing as they boiled in their sockets. He couldn't tell if his ears were burnt off or the next explosion had destroyed his hearing, but suddenly there was silence. All that was left to him was the sense of touch being melted off him as he fell into the small, dying sun at the heart of a doomed planet.

Wind.

That what it was. It was the wind. Lucas could feel the cold wind on his skin. He was grateful to no longer be burning, but it wasn't long before he began to feel cold and shiver. Little by little, he realized that he could hear again, though the only sound was the roar of the same wind pebbling his skin with goose flesh. He wondered, too, if he would ever see again until he grasped that his eyes were closed. As terrified to stay ignorant of what was going on as he was to know, he slowly opened them.

The underwater city and the inferno that had ended it were gone. He was falling through the sky over a large island peppered with tiny villages and farms. There was something vaguely familiar about the geography, but Lucas couldn't quite put his finger on it.

Aside from the wind, he became aware of a strange buzzing noise. Looking around, he spied a bird with rapid wing movements like those of a hummingbird. It landed on his outstretched palm, and when it folded its wings, Lucas saw it was again Star. She was tiny and weighed nothing in his hand. Her arms were two sets of wings that met at her naked shoulders, and her legs bent backwards, ending in prehensile claws. Gently she walked up his arm to sit on his shoulder, and once again, began a tale.

"The people here are very strange," she said. "They are more like ants than humans in that there is one queen and many children. Look closely at the island. What do you see?"

Lucas gazed at the mass rushing toward him, but the pattern he sought was still moving just out of his mental reach. It didn't look volcanic to him like most islands he'd seen. There were two hilly peaks and one strange land bridge that looked like it should be impossible. It was also weirdly symmetrical, leading from the narrow fingers of beach in the south to an enormous rounded dome at the north with lush grassland in between them. The dome... there was something about the dome and the cast of the hollows on its face.

The island was a woman.

She was huge and overgrown with trees and animals and life, but once Lucas realized it, he couldn't unsee it. At the edges of his vision in the distance, he spotted other similar masses shaped like women lying on their sides, on their backs, or sitting cross-legged in the sea. All immobile and silent and all serving as the homes of everything that lived on land in this world.

"Yes," chirped Star. "Here, all children come from the land. Babies are born in special groves. Most are female and nearly all are sterile. All the males who are born are expected to make a pilgrimage to the womb once in their lives to mate with the land. Not all do because it is a taxing experience that ages them before their time, but most are glad to be a part of the continuation of their world. Once in every generation or so, a fertile female will be born and cared for. They, too, will grow to enormous size and one day stride into the sea to become a new land themselves. In this way has Melia been colonized.

211

"The problem here is war. War for many reasons. Some wage it over religion, others for purity, and all for control in the end. Despite these islands being each their own bountiful land, the pattern replays over and over again as the years pass.

"First, someone will use violence to enforce their will. The death toll will require new conscripts to be born. At first, the land complies and births more of her children, but soon, men are forced at gunpoint to copulate again and again with the land to meet the demand for more warriors. The men, bodies wrecked, sick and old, often die anyway once they're used up.

"The groves of children become targets. Boys as young as seven are dragged off to their service, while girls even younger are taught to kill their sisters. The rare queen becomes a pawn, often fought over and rarely living to adulthood. Fields of sprouting children are burned, and the very earth around them grows brown and cracked as fighting destroys their home. Eventually, as a last, desperate act, the land itself will spontaneously reabsorb all her children to try and heal herself, only to be left barren and alone to die as the eons pass.

"It's slightly different all over this world, but it happens and happens and happens. One day, the final queen will gorge on her own abusive offspring to try and save herself. It won't be tomorrow or even a hundred years from now, but bit by bit, these people are raping themselves to extinction without a single clue how they are doing it."

The bird Star finished her history and took wing into the sky above him. Lucas turned and looked at her as she flew away, losing her in the blinding light of Melia's sun. Scared and alone again, he turned earthward and with a sickening feeling in his stomach, saw he was quite close to the ground now. Trees with broken branches reached up to impale him, and directly below, a field of large, pink flowers was spread out. With impact approaching, he screamed in terror and was barely surprised when the flowers turned to look at him in surprise at the noise. He closed his eyes against the coming crash, and his last thought before blackness took him was an apology to the children he would surely crush in his approaching death.

***

Gravel pressed painfully against Lucas's face, jarring him awake again. He sat up quickly to find himself on a city rooftop. All around and below him were the sounds of cars honking and people talking. It was a safe sound and he felt relief since the first moment Star had walked into his house.

Getting to his feet, he was grateful for not being hurled through the air or sea toward a doom, but now he wondered where the hell he was.

"This one is mine," said a voice.

Lucas turned and sitting on the edge of the building with her back toward him and her legs dangling into space was Star. Cautiously, he walked over to her to see what weird form she would inhabit this time.

This Star was just a girl. Probably a teenager or in her early twenties. She was slight with dark hair and dressed rather stereotypically Goth. It gave her an air of naïveté and youthful

213

melodrama, but her eyes were so old and full of pain, it was difficult to look into them. Nonetheless, she smiled and patted the space next to her for Lucas to sit.

"What do you mean, 'this one is yours?'" he asked.

Star took a deep breath and replied, "This world is mine. This is the one I ended. Look down there, see?"

Following her finger, Lucas spied a gir,l who looked very much like Star, standing in the street with a strange, terrifying-looking woman. They seemed to be arguing.

"She, well, me, is about to open the sky and unleash every horror imaginable on Earth. The sun will turn black, and demons will devour all of humanity, and everything is going to burn."

"Why the hell would you do something like that?" he asked. "That's awful."

Star shrugged. "It's not about right or wrong, really," she said. "It's about what is and what isn't. I had a boyfriend who had some difficulty letting go of me after we broke up, so he started messing with some things that he shouldn't. Ended up connecting with a force that really, really didn't like the idea of a man trying to reclaim a woman against her will because something like that had happened to her a long time ago. Long story short, everyone did their best to do the right thing, but it was all so messed up and terrible that world ended. If it hadn't been me, it probably would have been someone else eventually. Life's funny like that."

Lucas didn't know what to say. He wasn't sure if any of this was real. Did he drown in the tub and this was the afterlife? Was he dead? He didn't feel dead, not that he had any idea what death felt like anyway.

Below in the street, it was starting. Portals opened, and unspeakable things poured out in hordes. Car honks turned to screams, and the smell of spilled blood filled the air. Star stood up on the ledge of the building and looked down at him.

"Here's something I want you to think about - the world is merely a collection of points of view. Each of us creates what's around us, whether it's the places you and I fell through or this particular Earth or your home.

"The worst thing that you can do is remove someone's ability to create the world as a safe, stable place. It's worse than killing them because then they at least survive as a memory. When men and women go about removing the choices of others, removing their humanity and replacing it with a mirror to their own desire for sex and power, it's like pulling a brick out of a wall. Don't worry, it's a very big wall, and it's very strong. But if enough people do it once a day for long enough, the wall will crumble, and the void will take back the world from our sight."

"What does this have to do with me?" screamed Lucas over the end of the world.

Star grinned and pointed across the street to the brick building on the other side. In the red bricks, subtle shadings painted a picture of his wife's tear-streaked face. One by one, bricks fell out from the wall until there was only a swirling blackness shot through with red lightning. Suddenly, Lucas felt pulled toward it. He tried to climb back on the other side of the ledge, but the force was too strong. Scrambling, he gripped the cement as he dangled sideways over the maw.

Unaffected by the pull, Star hopped down and looked into his eyes. Her smile was warm, and Lucas almost begged her to help him.

"You're good people, Lucas," she said and unbelievably, reached out a hand to ruffle his hair. "But you need to be careful. All bad people started out as good people, and even once they became rotten, they still thought they were good. One hundred percent of them. That's how the world ends - with people standing around looking confused."

"Please," he said, fingers losing their grip.

"And thank you," she replied cheekily. "For shopping with us today."

And with that, she turned and walked away from him, a black sun blazing over her head. He watched her until his grip finally failed, and he tumbled backward into the dark. It was whispering his name in his wife's voice. Screaming it at him.

***

"Luke!"

There was a stinging smack on his cheek, and suddenly Lucas couldn't breathe. His airways contracted, and he felt water rushing out of his throat, raw and earthy with the bath salts. The room was so bright he couldn't see, and his chest heaved for oxygen as rainbows flashed across his vision.

"Luke! Lucas! Honey, are you okay?"

The blurs finally subsided, and a particularly dark blob began to look something like Suveda. He reached for her, but his legs slipped in the water, and he ended up draped over the edge of the tub. Uncontrollably, he heaved again, and more water and bile poured out of his mouth to puddle on the white mat. The strange hues of the bath and his bodily fluids stained it an impossible color.

Suddenly, he felt cool hands on his back, rubbing them. Suveda was patting him, cooing over him, trying to see if he was alright. It was nice. God, it was so nice.

"Can you get out?" asked Suveda.

Lucas tried to croak an answer but was reduced to weakly nodding. Suveda reached over and grabbed the chair from her vanity and pulled it over. Between leaning on it and her, Lucas managed to get up and out of the water, collapsing in the chair as he drank air in huge gulps. He closed his eyes to make the dizziness stop and for a time, just sat enjoying the process of breathing. It felt amazing, just to breathe.

Once he felt a little stronger, he opened his eyes and looked at his wife. She was in one of her business suits, though it was now soaking wet and probably ruined from helping him out. He would buy her a new one.

"What happened?" she asked. "Did you fall asleep in the tub? I got home and couldn't find you, and when I came in here, you were completely under the water. Did you hit your head or take some cold medicine or drink too much or… or… Jesus, Luke, you scared the

217

shit out of me! I thought you were dead. I thought maybe you'd k-killed yourself or something."

Suveda started crying as the adrenaline from pulling him from under the water backwashed into her system, and terrible ideas that had been suppressed started flooding out. In between sobs, Lucas could hear her blaming herself and cursing herself for hitting him and accusing him of hurting her. Soon, her litany of crimes against herself was coming so rapidly Lucas couldn't tell them apart from one another.

He reached out weakly, grabbing her shoulder. He pulled, but the gesture was not really to embrace her because he could barely lift his arms. It was just an indicator he would dearly like to hold her. Suveda leaned into him, and he laid his head against her.

"Thank you," he whispered.

***

Suveda insisted on driving him to an emergency care clinic to get checked out. Lucas wanted to protest but didn't have the energy. He had a bad moment, when his wife was helping him dress, with a flashback of Star preparing him for whatever had taken place. It sent him into a twitching, crying jag that required Suveda to lie down beside him and stroke his hair until he calmed down. Finally, he was able to walk meekly to the car and step up into the SUV. He was grateful for the strap to lean on.

Suveda was quiet for a minute as they drove, and the rocking of the car on the road was soothing Lucas until he was nearly asleep. He jerked awake when she finally spoke.

"What happened, Luke?" she asked. "I've been calling you for days. You didn't answer when I landed, and I figured you were just busy or something, but then I didn't hear from you that night or the next. In fact, Tony from the Champion Forest store called me to ask where you were because you missed some sort of meeting. I was worried sick. Your dad didn't know where you were. No one knew. I don't want to badger you right now, but please tell me something."

Lucas stared into the night's traffic, trying to piece it all together. The date on the car radio was three days later than it should have been. There was no evidence in the bathroom Star had ever been there except for the brightly colored water Suveda found him in. Apparently, Suveda never called her in any case, though it didn't explain why he had missed his wife's call in the first place. He idly wondered if Star had fed the cat.

"I don't remember," was all he said in the end. "I took a bath, and the next thing I knew, you were pulling me out of it. That's it, really. I don't know what happened."

"Maybe you had an allergic reaction or something," she said. Lucas shrugged. Maybe he had, and everything from the ritual to the end of the worlds he'd witnessed was a fever dream.

Something itched at the back of his head, and Lucas idly scratched at it. He was surprised to find something there, caught in his hair. He gingerly pulled at it, yanking out a few small black hairs in the process. In the passing street lights, he looked at what had been stuck to him. It was small and hard, a crystal with a strange smell and a small tangle of pink flowers that seemed to breathe. One turned to look at him and Lucas struggled to suppress a scream as Star's laugh pounded in his ears. He thought about throwing it out the window but wondered if the doctors might want to test it. Hands shaking, he put it into his jacket pocket.

The emergency clinic was slow when they got there. Suveda led Lucas to a chair and went to fill out the forms needed to get him seen. Doctors' offices depressed Lucas greatly. It always seemed like, unless you were pregnant, no one ever went to one happy. Everyone always waited until they were at death's door to go looking for care. They were rotten places as far as he was concerned, even if necessary.

The man sitting next to him was talking on the phone, hissing his words as if he wanted to yell, but didn't dare to. He held his phone awkwardly in his left hand, as if he wasn't used to doing so, and his right was wrapped in a red-stained dishtowel, like he'd cut himself on something quite badly.

"Cassandra," he said. "You better listen to me, Cassandra. I mean it this time. I'm here at the emergency room. Do you hear me, the emergency room and this is all your fault. If you'd come home when you said you would have, then I wouldn't have cut myself just trying to make a damn sandwich. You're supposed to be my wife."

Cassandra… the name tickled Lucas's mind. Something Suveda said about a woman at her shelter and a man with a gun.

"This is over," he hissed harder. "No more games with you. You're always playing games with me, trying to get me to do what you want through all this passive-aggressive bullshit. It's abuse.

You're abusing me. I'm bleeding to death because of your stupid abuse, but no one is going to believe that because men can't be abused. They believe you when you lie about me, even though there's never been a mark on you. Not like me with this bleeding hand."

Lucas rolled his head to the side to look at the man. He was blond and well-built. Handsome the way a well-bred dog is handsome. Still, the whining tone of his voice made him appear young and weak. Listening to his circular attacks was making Lucas's skin crawl. The man noticed Lucas watching him and gave him a very direct "fuck off, buddy" look before turning in his seat away from Lucas and taking a sip of his coffee with his injured hand.

With the man making increasingly more ridiculous accusations into the phone, Lucas reached over quietly and took the man's Styrofoam cup without being seen. With his other hand, he reached into his pocket and pulled out the crystal, watching the flowers twist in his hand and nuzzle against his palm. He thought long and hard about what he'd seen under the water, the stories Star told and the pain they cause.

His mouth was dry, but he managed to work up just enough saliva to launch a couple of drops onto the crystal. It quietly hissed a little, a sound that could have been mistaken for the distant noise of a respirator. Lucas tipped the crystal into the man's coffee cup, using his finger to stir it until it dissolved. The liquid was scalding hot, but Lucas barely felt it. He just enjoyed the wonderful scents of cookies and fresh cut hay and pus that wafted up into the air as a result. He breathed deeply and then quietly set the cup down within the man's easy reach.

His eyes closed again, and Lucas drifted on dream waves. Out of the corner of his hearing, he heard the man take a sip of his drink between his rage-filled litanies. Was it the same man who'd threatened his wife at Suveda's shelter? Lucas didn't really think it mattered. Star had said something like, "If it wasn't him, it would have just been someone else." Some other bad guy convinced he was the hero or the victim until the world fell down around him.

"You have to be careful about that sort of thing," mumbled Lucas to himself. "Never know where it might lead."

Everybody's Waitin' for the Man with the Bag

Jamie walked along the side of the road. He was cold, but stubborn ten-year-old pride wouldn't let him put on the bright orange jacket he was carrying by his side. His dad had insisted he take it with him, otherwise he might get sick. Jamie rather bitterly admitted that he might have slightly overestimated his resistance to exposure, but this was a matter of principle! Besides, the store wasn't far.

Christmas was a day away, though Jamie was far too old for any baby stuff about Santa Claus and reindeer. He was happy enough to get the presents, so long as his parents followed his list. They always ended up adding something else "From Santa" under the tree. Usually something small and practical. Actually, that little MP3 player last year had been pretty sweet. It was pre-loaded with audio books and *Doctor Who* radio plays so they wouldn't take up space in his phone. Of course, they could have just gotten him a phone with a bigger memory, but it did make walks like these more of a pleasant outing than a chore. His earbuds buzzed with time travel adventures.

Jamie smiled. Hopefully, they would be done at Grandma's in time to get home and watch the Christmas special tomorrow.

Far enough from his house, where he was certain his dad couldn't see him, Jamie shrugged into his coat. He was so happy to find his dad had stuck mittens in the pockets, he almost forgot to be annoyed for the condescending treatment. Didn't he know that he could take care of himself?

The walk to the nearby store wasn't blessed with a sidewalk, and Jamie's feet were cold from the soggy grass. His mother was working at the hospital tonight so she could spend Christmas Day with them, and that left all the cooking and cleaning and last minute Christmas errands to his father. Jamie's dad was a pretty good guy, even occasionally cool when he wasn't being embarrassing, but he had a very deadline-driven approach to everything that usually left him scrambling to finish. Hence, Jamie's regular trips to pick up ingredients and supplies his father had forgotten.

Jamie didn't mind, really. He liked getting out of the house, even if it was cold. Most of his friends from school had out of town Christmas plans, and the ones that didn't were all busy hosting relatives who had come in. There wasn't much to do as far as having a good time, and all his video games were old and stupid, since his parents wouldn't buy him anything with Christmas coming up. He might act put upon, but this was heaps better than listening to his dad talk to himself as he moved back and forth through the kitchen and dining room.

He finally reached the first of the shopping centers that abutted the series of apartment complexes he called home. The walk to the store was a little less than a mile round trip, but it was a strange walk. Half of it was a grassy field next to the little compartmental building of the complex, and the other half was like a little miniature city. Still, it was well-lit and safe enough that Jamie had been fetching things for his dad for a year now.

Over the sounds of The Doctor and Charley Pollard running from Cybermen, Jamie noticed a loud, ringing noise. He pulled his earbuds out to make sure there wasn't an ambulance or something coming toward him and was relieved to see it was just a woman dressed as Santa ringing a hand bell and holding up a pail for donations. The sign next to her urged people to give for those who had nothing, and Jamie figured he'd drop the change from his purchases into her bucket. It was a nice thing to do.

The ringing got louder and more annoying as he walked toward her. She was between the pharmacy and the grocery, a prime place to pick up people running errands. The Girl Scouts did the same thing with their cookie stands each year. Jamie wanted to put his earbuds back in, but he didn't want to look like a jerk.

"Merry Christmas, young man," said the woman. "Make a donation?"

Up close, Jamie didn't really like the look of the woman. She was very large and doughy, her mouth a nearly round hole between her puffed cheeks. The Santa suit fit her frame admirably, but the cheap, white wig and hat looked clownish over her visible black bangs sticking out from underneath them. She smelled like cooking wine, and one arm was bandaged with a dirty wrapping.

"I'll drop in my change when I get back from the store," he promised.

"God bless you, handsome," she said with an unpleasant wink. "I'll be waiting here."

Jamie walked on, thinking the woman was a little creepy. He plugged in once more and was grateful to enter the store and its warmth. He shopped quickly from the list his dad had made and then wandered around looking at Christmas stuff while he waited for the audio story to end. A buzzing in his pocket alerted him of a text from his dad, asking him if he was okay and reminding him he needed the tomatoes and peppers within the next half hour or so. Jamie replied he was on his way back, paid at the register, and walked back out with his sack of groceries.

Heading back, he spied the woman with the bell again and awkwardly tried to switch the heavy sack to one arm while digging in his jeans for the change with his other. The operation wasn't going very smoothly, and soon he was just standing in front of her fumbling like a juggler who had forgotten how to juggle. Exasperated, he yanked out his earbuds again and set the bag on the ground to free up his hands. The woman laughed in a way that was probably meant to be kindly but sounded mean in Jamie's ears.

Finally, he extracted all of sixty-four cents for his troubles, and the woman once again passed along the blessings of God. This time, she called him "Tiger" and Jamie didn't like it any better. He bent to pick up his groceries but stopped, staring at the sidewalk.

He'd missed it when he'd come by the first time, but now, in the low afternoon light, he couldn't keep his eyes off it. In colored chalk was a picture of a large man with a bag draped over his back. It wasn't Santa, though. This man's skin was black, with red eyes. Instead of a Coca-Cola red suit, he wore rags, and goat horns grew from his forehead. His mouth was open, and a long, pink tongue snaked out.

"What the heck is that?" asked Jamie before he could stop himself.

"That, Tiger, is the Krampus," said the woman giggling a high-pitched giggle. "You ever heard of the Krampus?"

"No," said Jamie. He was sorry he'd said anything.

"He's like the dark Santa Claus," said the woman. "While Santa is out giving presents to good boys and girls, Krampus is out leaving switches and belts in the stockings of the bad ones so their parents will have something to beat them with. If a boy or girl was particularly bad, Krampus would pop them in his sack and take him or her with him home to eat. That's how you got kids to mind back in the old days. You had to teach them respect. Most parents are too scared of political correctness these days to correct their kids properly. I see them all the time, going back and forth without showing me, their elder, the proper respect. You seem really good, though, donating your change and talking like you should. Surprised you don't know about Krampus. Suppose he doesn't get much work these days. Everyone's too damned liberal."

Jamie was at a loss. He'd never heard this story, and his parents had damn sure never spanked him, let alone hit him with a belt. He wondered what a switch was. Like a light switch? Why would you hit someone with that?

Whatever the case, he wanted to get the hell away from this weird woman and go home. So he wished her a Merry Christmas and added a "Ma'am" for good measure, then walked past her with the ringing of her bell following him. It wasn't until the ringing was out of earshot he felt safe putting his story back on, but honestly, it had lost some of its appeal. Fish-people in 23rd-century Venice wasn't very scary anymore. He couldn't get the graffiti out of his head, and it wasn't until he was almost at his own doorstep that he realized what was bothering him.

His shoes kept squelching in soggy, unpaved ground from last night's rain, but the sidewalk had been dry enough for a clear, chalk drawing. That woman must have drawn it. What a weirdo.

"Dad, I'm home," shouted Jamie, as he came through the door. "I got everything you asked for!'

His dad rounded the corner from the kitchen and took the bag. He was a small man who buzzed with energy. Jamie quickly handed him the sack and watched, amused, as his dad sprinted back to the kitchen. Leaning in the doorway, he admired his father's typical and insane manner of putting the groceries away as he dumped everything on the floor and hurled items left and right into their proper places. One day, Jamie hoped he'd have that dexterity. Even when the loaf of bread his dad had tossed onto the counter started to slide off, he managed to catch it in one hand and toss it back in place while putting away a tin of rosemary in the other on the same motion.

"Crap!" his dad shouted, as he suddenly ground two cans of beans into his eye sockets. "Crappity crap crap dammit dammit crap!"

"What?" asked Jamie.

"Potatoes," his dad said. "I forgot to tell you potatoes. I need red potatoes for the mashed potatoes. And milk."

Jamie saw where this was going.

"Couldn't you just use some instant mashed potatoes?" he asked. "We've got some. I saw them yesterday. Gran won't even notice."

His dad removed the cans from his eyes and let his arms dangle while he stared at his son with his head cocked. A silent couple of seconds ticked by.

"Well, she won't," pleaded Jamie.

"And how many of your Christmas presents would you like to wager on that hypothesis?" asked his father. "Hmmmmm?"

Jamie had to admit that his Gran would probably notice. She wouldn't say anything overt about it, but he'd probably hear a lot of comments about how it was a shame his mom wasn't around as much to help out at the house and maybe if she was, then his dad wouldn't be so stressed for time to cook and...

Yeah. Dad needed potatoes. And milk. Jamie sighed.

"Look, Jamiroquai," he said, using one of those completely inexplicable pet names he seemed to have an endless supply of. "I'd drive over myself and do it really quick if I could, but this stuff has to be tended. The roast is coming out in ten, and that sauce needs stirring, etcetera, etcetera ad infinitum. I promise this is the last trip today. Anything else, I'll just endure the wrath. C'mon, help me out?"

Jamie made a big show of putting his mittens back on and dramatically holding out his hand for twenty dollars. His dad crossed his palm with paper money, and Jamie turned to leave. Suddenly, his dad hugged him from behind.

"I appreciate it, Jamie," he said. "I really do. Why don't you get yourself a dessert or something with the change, and we'll let you open a present tonight when Mom gets home. And I swear we will leave Gran's in time to get home for *Doctor Who* tomorrow, okay?'

"Alright, alright," said Jamie, shrugging out of the hug. "I'll take care of it for you. Last trip, though. If you think of anything else you need, you've got about fifteen minutes to text it to me."

"Yes, Commodore," said his dad. "Try to hurry. I'm worried about the dark and the road."

"I know," said Jamie. "I'll go fast."

Back outside, the sun was already hidden behind the buildings, and the streetlights were starting to come on. The temperature was also dropping dramatically, and Jamie briefly thought about going back in for his hat real quick. Instead, he zippered up his jacket and began another trudge to the store.

Cars with their headlights on streaked past him. Jamie didn't like to admit it, but he was a little worried, too. For as long as he could remember, his dad had pounded in the fact that holidays were full of drunk drivers having too good a time to notice they were so blitzed that they were a danger to themselves and others. It was one of the reasons he had this stupid orange (but thankfully, very warm) coat in the first place. It made him easier to see, but he was always very mindful of the fact that any one of these cars could have a drunk behind the wheel, ready to jump the curb and take out anything in their path.

He edged a little farther from the road, even if it did take him into slushier ground. He hoped someone had gotten him proper rain boots for Christmas and congratulated himself on such adult a thought.

Wanting to pay attention to the road, he refrained from putting on another story until he'd reached the shopping center and the safety of the paved sidewalk in front of the stores. He flipped through the MP3 player to find a Christmas tale. This one was about a house that came to life and endlessly replayed a murder mystery on Christmas Eve. One of his favorites.

Lost in the tale, he had forgotten about the donations woman until he almost blundered into her. She was packing up her pail and things. The stores were all closing in the next half hour, and he guessed she was on her way home. At her feet, the Krampus still leered up into the night sky. Jamie saw her say something at him with another unpleasant smile, but he didn't want to interrupt the story.

"Forgot some things for my dad," he said loudly, walking past her. "Got to get them quick before the store's closed. Merry Christmas!"

With a wave, he turned his back, and walked quickly away from her. There wasn't time to chat, and she freaked him out anyway.

The clerks and stock staff were already tending to their closing duties, hoping to get out of the building as soon as possible. The meat department was all packed up and washed, the deli shut down, and the florist already had her coat on and was playing on her phone until the call to leave came in. There were just enough red potatoes for his dad's recipe, milk to spare, and Jamie took a few minutes to help himself to a big tin of Christmas candy.

"I should get you to text me your shopping list," said the manager, who liked the boy who was in so often for his forgetful dad. "We could compare notes and maybe you wouldn't need to make two trips."

"Nah, I'm okay," said Jamie. "It's a short walk, and it gets me out of the house."

"Not to be all candy from strangers or anything, but it's getting cold and dark," said the manager. "Would you like a lift home? We're going to have the lights off in ten minutes."

"I'll be home by then," said Jamie. The man was nice enough, but years of stranger-danger leaves kids habitually prone to erring on the side of caution when it comes to adults. Besides, he'd done this a hundred times.

"Okay, Jamie," said the manager. "Be safe and happy holidays."

"You, too," replied Jamie and he turned to walk out.

Night comes quickly in winter, and for a second, Jamie thought seriously about going back inside and taking the manager up on his offer of a ride. He wasn't scared, of course. Not at all, but it was cold and dark, and there were drunks on the road. He was still thinking about it when the lights went off behind him. Now, there were only pools of hazy illumination from the weak streetlights. It was weird how they seemed to be too high up in the air for the light to get all the way down to the ground.

That's stupid, thought Jamie. With a snort, he gripped his shopping bag and started walking quickly home. The shops were all shuttered, and only a few managers and employees were hurrying through the parking lot under hoods and hats to leave behind the whole working mess and spend time with their families. The only one on the sidewalk was Jamie, hurriedly skulking home.

Something about the night was getting to him. He couldn't put his finger on it, but it was putting him on edge. The sky above was overcast and let down no light from the stars or the moon. The air was electric with cold, and the gate to the complex looked like it was on the other side of the planet. Every car that cruised by sounded like it was cutting the wind with a knife, almost like the evening itself was screaming.

"C'mon, get it together," Jamie said to himself. He was a big kid. Practically an adult. Being afraid of the dark was for babies.

He had just passed the store when he noticed a light off to his right. It was a bright and warm light, but faint. He paused for a second until he realized he was standing on the face of the Krampus drawn on the sidewalk. Weirded out, he moved off, but when he did so, the bag of groceries loudly ripped. The potatoes and milk hit the sidewalk with a soft thud, but the tin of candy made a loud banging noise. Jamie dropped to his knees quickly to try and gather up his belongings. He cursed himself for forgetting the canvas bags his mom was always on him to use. Better for the environment anyway.

The sound of shuffling feet startled him, and Jamie looked up. The donation woman was standing over him, grinning down.

"Need some help there, Tiger?" she said with her lips stretched thin over her teeth.

"N-no, I've got it," said Jamie.

"Are you sure?" she said. "Maybe I've got another bag back here. You want another bag?"

Jamie really didn't. He wanted to go home right now, even if it meant carrying his groceries awkwardly. The woman stepped over him and scooped up the tin of candy that he'd dropped. She looked at it while licking her lips.

"Come on, Tiger," she said. "I've got lots of stuff to help you. You being so nice and all."

And with that, she reached down and grabbed Jamie under one arm to hoist him up. The gesture felt anything but friendly, and her grip was like iron as she pushed him toward the alley between the grocery store and the drug store. Jamie stumbled to keep his feet, and around the corner was a small barrel full of burning trash. The woman's donation bucket and other items were stuffed into a loaded shopping cart that was stacked with wrapped plastic bags full of items until it was taller than she was. On the ground next to it was a filthy sleeping bag.

Jamie turned, but the woman blocked the alley behind him. She was reaching into the candy tin and happily sampling some of the chocolates, loudly licking her fingers by shoving them one by one as deep into her mouth as she could before slowly withdrawing them. The gesture was beyond gross.

"There're sacks in that bag hanging on the end," she said. "Go on and get you one."

Jamie hurried over past the fire and snatched one out of the bag. As quickly as he could, he stuffed the potatoes and the milk in and turned to walk away. The woman was leaning against the brick wall with his candy.

"You sure you don't want to stay and keep a girl company?" she asked, dark chocolate smeared around her mouth. "I'm all alone on Christmas. Lonely and cold and looking for someone to talk to. There just aren't any boys like you that walk past me, these days. Nice, sweet boys that show an elder the proper respect."

Jamie was pretty much beyond speaking now. He just shook his head and started almost sprinting past her. He thought he made it when her hand grabbed him around the collar of his jacket and yanked. He stumbled backward and fell next to the burning barrel. In the firelight, she looked huge and ogrish. She was still licking her lips.

"You didn't say, 'thank you' for the bag," she said. "I thought you were a good boy."

"Th-th-th-th-"

"Oh, sure, now you say thanks," said the woman. "Little shits like you always remember your manners when you're reminded. I shouldn't have to remind you. You should just know."

The woman reached down to her waist and unbuckled the wide, leather strap of a belt for her Santa suit. Free from support, her pants fell down around her ankles, and she stepped out of them. Her legs

237

were hairy and smeared with things Jamie didn't want to know about. In her hand, she wrapped the belt tightly and then swung hard. The buckle clanged against the barrel, and Jamie covered his head and screamed. The sound came again and again and again until he was sobbing.

Once again, the woman reached down and hauled him to his feet. She brought her face close to his and licked him up the side of his face. Her breath was rancid and vile, only bearable thanks to the candy she'd taken from him. She started whispering in his ear.

"You're going to learn something now," she growled. "You're going to learn how to treat a lady like me and what happens to you if you don't."

With one hand, she reached down and started fumbling at his jeans. Trembling like a leaf, he weakly slapped at her hands but was powerless against the adult. He was crying and frightened, and he just wanted to go home.

Suddenly, a new sound filled the alley. It was hard to describe, but Jamie could have sworn someone had just ripped off a very large adhesive bandage. The ripping noise bounced around the stone alley like a ricocheting bullet, and for a moment, the woman stopped her attack while still holding him too tight to escape. She was a beast of a human, this woman, and something of the beast in her knew there was danger. She glanced left and right, searching for the source.

Jamie was still shaking so hard it was like a seizure, and it took him a minute to realize it wasn't just fear. Cold had descended even harder than it already was. Above him, fat snowflakes began to fall, and out of nowhere, a heap of snow came crashing down to douse the firelight. Everything went dark.

He felt himself being flung aside and collapsed against the wall. The woman turned and pulled a long, serrated kitchen knife from under her sleeping bag. She was still naked from the waist down but didn't seem to mind either the cold or the dark. She was ready to fight, not flee.

"Who's out there?" she shouted. "I don't have a problem with you. Just leave a poor woman alone, or you'll be shitting out of a hole in your stomach."

The only answer was a low growl and a huge rustle. The snow was falling thicker now. Jamie looked up at the woman, half obscured by the sudden curtain of falling snow. It had quickly covered his mittens, but he noticed that it didn't smell anything like the usual dirty, wet stuff that came from the city's skies. Nervously, he held his hands under his nose and sniffed them.

It wasn't snow, it was chalk. Ice cold chalk, but still chalk.

Ahead of him, a shadow detached itself from the others. It seemed to be blackness itself moving until Jamie had the sense to look further up. The shape was easily twenty feet tall, and its eyes were narrow and red and mad. Against the sky, Jamie could make out huge, curved horns. Across the shape's back, something that pulsed and writhed was held in a large sack. With a grunt, it was slung from over the shape's shoulder and landed on the ground with a strange clicking noise.

The woman seemed taken aback for just a second. The Krampus shadow growled low again.

"You're nothing," she whispered. "You're nothing!"

She sprang toward the Krampus with her knife held out in front of her, only for a huge, swatting blow to knock her completely out of the way. The knife flew up into the air and clanged to the ground beside Jamie. He dove for it and held it out in front of him, still afraid to move.

The woman groaned on the ground, trying to get up. Fast as dark follows light, the Krampus shadow moved over her, dragging her up into the air with one powerful arm. There she dangled, legs kicking and spitting at the beast that held her. Rather than a growl, this time it roared, an old sound of the woods and the tundra that froze prey with fear in its tracks.

Leaning down, the Krampus used his other hand to untie the sack he'd laid on the ground. The opening yawned wide, and inside it, Jamie could see skulls. So many tiny, child-sized skulls. Each one had a small, tallow candle where previously the brain had been, and the teeth had been removed. In their places had been driven all manners of sharp things; discarded razor blades, broken glass, pointed shells and rusty saw edges. Exposed to the night sky, the skulls began snapping and biting, leaping like starving piranha at the dangling woman above them. Jamie put his hands to his ears to block the infernal clicking noise their movements produced.

His terrible bag ready to receive, the Krampus reached up and grabbed the top of the woman's Santa suit. With a disgusted, bull-like snort, he ripped it from her body, leaving her nude in the night. He toppled her wig and hat off her head with a dismissive flick of his claw. Jamie wanted to close his eyes, but even the ability to blink seemed to have been taken from him.

With another roar, the Krampus hoisted the woman up high by the neck and slammed her down into the sack of biting skulls. Her screams were muffled under the weight of them, but the sack jerked and kicked as they bit into the woman's flesh. The Krampus looked down into the writhing mess, and his long tongue rolled out of his mouth as the struggle continued.

Finally, there was silence and the motions stopped. The Krampus withdrew his arm and held a fresh skull, picked clean. He turned and hurled the thing into the wall where it shattered into bone dust.

And then he looked at Jamie.

What expression was on the Krampus's face was impossible to tell. Only his red eyes could be seen, though the fire had gone from a blaze to a low yellow. Jamie watched him reach down to tie up his bag once again. He hoped he would be spared the woman's terrible fate, but the creature started toward him, and Jamie finally fainted from the fear as each pounding footstep drew nearer.

***

Crunch.

Crunch.

Crunch.

Jamie was edging back into consciousness. For a second, his mind thought the sound he heard was that of small skulls eating him in savory bites. Then he wondered if he was a skull, consuming others with mindless abandon as he listened to the sound of his own teeth cut through sinew and crack through bone.

But it was only the sound of footsteps on gravel. He was being carried in someone's arms. He allowed his eyes to crack open, seeing the color of blue and the word "POLICE." His hand darted to his pocket where his MP3 player, full of safe stories about blue police boxes and happy adventures, was still sitting. He rubbed it like a talisman.

Whoever was carrying him finally stopped and awkwardly shifted Jamie to one arm so he could knock. It was his own door.

"Hello?" said his father. "Dear God, what happened?"

Jamie felt himself being given over to his dad, and he clutched at him and wept. They collapsed on the couch together, his father's intricate cooking ritual forgotten in his terror. Jamie sobbed out incoherently until he was out of breath. He finally just allowed himself to be rocked in his dad's arms.

"What happened?" he asked.

"Your son had a nasty run-in," said the policeman. His voice was soft and romantic with just a touch of an Old World accent. "There was a woman posing as a donations collector down by the grocery store. She was just a vagrant with a con going on. Apparently, she also had a taste for young boys. Good thing I was on patrol down that way. I saw him get pulled into an alley and came running. The woman's gone, but I'll put out a bulletin tonight, and we'll keep an eye out to bag her. He doesn't seem hurt, but I'm no doctor."

Jamie's dad looked down at his son with a mix of terror and relief.

"Thank you, Officer..." he said.

The policeman paused for a moment, almost as if he didn't know the answer. He finally said, "McGann."

"McGann," replied Jamie's dad. "I don't know what would have happened if you hadn't been there."

"Really?" said the policeman. "I do. Rape. Death. New stories. Funerals. Stuff like that. Gory details aside, that's what would have happened. It's not my place to tell a man how to raise children, sir, but maybe the dead, dark of winter is not the place to be sending a boy out for the sake of a sack of potatoes? There are things in the dark, you know."

Jamie's dad hung his head.

"Still, no harm done, eh?" said the policeman. "He seems unhurt, though scared, of course. You'll want to go down and make a statement tomorrow, but not tonight. It's

Christmas Eve, after all. They'll have enough to deal with without someone not in immediate danger."

"I-" started his dad. The policeman raised his hand.

"No buts," he said. "I'd get the boy to bed if it were me. You'll want to call his mother and tell her everything. I'll be off. Who knows who else might be needing a hand tonight."

Jamie watched the big man who had carried him tip his hat to his dad and walk out of their house. For several minutes, his dad held him tightly, and for the first time in many years, Jamie was just grateful for the arms of his parent around him.

After the policeman left, Jamie's dad let loose his own torrent of sobs and apologies. They held each other for a long time before Jamie finally felt strong enough to tell his dad he wanted to go to bed. His dad nodded and set the boy down. Briefly, he returned to the kitchen to manage a few fires while Jamie pulled out clean pajamas from the warm dryer. He brushed his teeth and then allowed his dad to lead him up to bed. They said good night at the door, and Jamie went into his dark room.

There, in the corner near the window, sat the goat man, the dark saint of winter, the Krampus. He was cross-legged and huge, with his horns touching the ceiling. If Jamie turned his head just the right way, he could still see the illusion of the policeman that fooled his dad.

The Krampus was no shadow, but was neither fully there, either. Jamie could see the stitching in his clothes and the hair on his arms, but if he looked hard enough, he could see through these things to

245

the wall and posters behind him. The face was no black shade with burning eyes, but that of an old man. His beard was grey and full, and his was face lined with wrinkles. Even the horns looked commonplace on him.

Next to him was the bag.

The Krampus looked hard at the boy for a long while. In his eyes seemed to be reflected a sadness and a loss that no human would ever live long enough to understand.

"Good evening, summer's child," said the Krampus in a voice low as lost valleys. "It has been a busy one, has it not?"

Jamie only nodded. In the distance, he could hear his father on the phone to his mother at the hospital, begging forgiveness for letting him go out by himself after dark. Jamie started to shake.

"Come to my arms, summer's child," said the Krampus. "Come sit and talk with me a while 'ere I move on."

Jamie moved slowly toward the giant, his brain full of the woman's grisly end. Nonetheless, the Krampus scooped him up gently and cradled the boy in his massive limbs. Jamie actually found himself relaxed, smelling the old, soft leather of the Krampus's clothes and the sharpness of fir trees that exuded from him.

"Knoweth me, summer's child?" asked the Krampus.

"She said you were something evil and mean," replied Jamie.

"Aye," said the Krampus. "That I am. Evil and cold and cruel and the worst of bad deaths is old Krampus. No wonder that meat-rot knew of me. Like is like, after all, but fear nothing of old Krampus,

246

summer's child. Long has it been since brave hearts and good hearts have beat against my skin. I would simply enjoy it if you would allow."

Jamie nodded sleepily.

"What do you call who comes tonight?" asked the Krampus. "The man with the bag. The not-me. Say his name."

"Santa," said Jamie. "Saint Nicholas."

"Hmmmn," growled the Krampus. "Such small names you have for such things as the *jorgergdusandnii*. Not your fault. You are a small people. That is maybe why he loves you so. He is kind. So kind. It's said that it was he who brought you fire from the jealous heavens. Poor, punished giant who walks the wild frozen wastes.

"I know not, for he has not told me. We meet seldom, he and I, and I have forgotten much since the first meeting in the woods so many centuries ago. I am a beast still, though more than a just beast.

"He has wandered the world since you summer children were in your very infancy. When the cold descended and your grandfathers retreated to caves to hide from the winter's wrath, he was there. He found lost children and brought them home. He provided gifts of food and skins and other things less important, but no less appreciated when the nights were so long, they seemed to have no end. Always invisible. Always glimpsed in passing. The last of the *snatitsegmonay* who would not allow the greatest of darkness to consume mankind. He would be light."

The Krampus felt a warmth envelope him as he recounted the history of winter to this child. Patience was not his strong point, but he recognized the need to remind humanity of what was at stake in the cold and dark. And he liked this boy, brave and foolish as he was. He remembered how he grabbed the fallen knife and he had watched him fight evil with courtesy at first. So like the *jorgergdusandnii* in that way.

"One day, he realized a terrible thing. He understood that where he brought his light, the darkness fled, and with it the things that preyed and struck from the darkness. Driven away, they would still come back to hunt his wards the moment his back was turned. What to do?

"Fearless, he went into the forests alone without light and found me, the greatest of the night beasts. We fought and should you ever look upon his true face, you will see it covered in scars of my making. But he tamed me, brought me to heel, and in doing so, he cured me of my bestial dumbness. From there, he set me to haunt the dark where he could not go. I was to be the terror that terrors fear, and so I am, summer's child."

The Krampus hugged the boy tightly. All beasts long for touch and affection and love. That was how man tamed them, by playing on their need for a higher hand to tell them they were worthy. The Krampus was long past such necessity, but he envied the love his master received sometimes.

"I hunt children," he said. "I do, but I hunt those the winds tell me will become knives in the dark. I seek those whose childish sadism will grow into adult atrocity. I can smell rot in a soul, and my bag is ready to receive them. It is my part in the design of my master, and I do not regret it.

"But too rarely are there nights like tonight, young child of summer, that I feel like the bringer of light. There is no need to thank me for your salvation. In many ways, you, young child, are my own."

His only reward for the outpouring was a small snore.

The beast smiled to himself. It was plenty that the boy had trusted him enough to fall asleep in his arms. More than he ever deserved. With slow gentleness, he reached over and laid the lad in his bed. He covered him with the warmest covers and took down the old teddy bear with one eye from the decorative shelf to give him something to hold in his sleep.

He threw his bag of nightmares out the window and clambered out of the opening himself. On the night wind, he smelled things. Somewhere, a young teenage boy was doing things to his sister that made her meat smell of suicide. Somewhere, another young girl was smothering her cat with a cold smile on her face as it died. The dawn was coming, but before it did, the Krampus had business in the dark corners of their rooms. He slung his sack over his shoulders and whistled a song of the woods at the falling snow.

Liner Notes

I have no idea what real writers call this section. Old punk that I am, I treat short story collections more like albums than books. So here are your liner notes.

In Neil Gaiman's *Sandman* series there's a short story that is, in and of itself, a collection of even shorter stories called "Parliament of Rooks". In it, he discusses the habit of rooks to descend in a circle with one bird in the center. That bird will caw and caw, and eventually the other birds will either fly off and leave him or rip him to pieces. Gaiman says the center bird is telling a story, and the response lets him know how the others liked it. I can think of no better analogy for being a writer, hence this first of six total *Rook Circles*. Hopefully you won't kill me at the end.

You can blame George R. R. Martin for **Underbite**. I was too broke to pick up the fifth Westeros book when it came out, so I had to settle for his vampire novel *Fevre Dream*. Great book, by the way, but in it, I heard the last straw of my least favorite trope - the vampire superiority monologue. It happens in every damned television show, film, comic, video game, you name it, and it is always complete and utter horseshit. A couple of characters to hold the rant later and here we are. That's a real scholarship fund I mention, though, in case you're looking for a place to donate money in the name of better dental health.

When my friend Jaidis Shaw was looking for submissions for her underwater horror anthology, *Lurking in the Deep*, I jumped at the chance. I'm a huge fan of terrors from the deep, but I literally could not think of a single thing that had not been done before. I was four-thousand words into a story before I realized I was retelling Clive Barker's "Scapegoats." Finally, I stumbled on the idea of a mechanical land shark gone mad for **A Senseless Eating Machine**.

The first non-cartoon I ever saw in a movie theater was *Jaws: The Revenge*, which my dad took me to after months of begging. It was, and remains, a stupid film, but the unbelievable and obviously fake shark scared me more than any real world footage. The idea that we could create a monster like that made me wonder what would ever happen if they should come to life. I guess we'll find out. The aquarium in Houston actually exists.

Nevaeh was hard to write. There really are drive-thru churches down the street from my house. Not like the ones I describe, but yeah, it's coming.

What became "Nevaeh" started out as a musical project for The Black Math Experiment. My keyboard player Chris and I thought up this idea called *Cold Charisma*, where we would pretend to be hired to soundtrack an indie film, complete some of the work, and then tell the press the film was cancelled after a fatal fire killed some of the cast. Never got around to finishing it, but Chris got some of the music done, and I outlined the basic story of a boy that steals a girl's body to have a Viking funeral. Years later, it's finally here.

When I set out to write **Ceridwen's Cauldron**, it was supposed to be a funny story about my wife's addiction to Lush bath products. Then, well, I got really involved in watching GamerGate and the new misogyny movement, and I went a little cuckoo. I really wanted to get into the minds of these terrible men in a way that didn't kill or destroy them, and this is the result.

Thanks to Carmilla Voiez for loaning me Star from her *Starblood* series. I never liked her apocalypse and wanted to give a character I'd grown to love something beyond the pain.

I hope to do a Christmas story in each collection. **Everybody's Waitin' for the Man with the Bag** might be the easiest thing I've ever written, having sprung up whole in three days. It's just a winter's tale, really. Nothing special, but it's my own exploration on the difference between what is evil and what is necessary. World's a hard place, and you have to learn that sometimes the choice is between what is barely bearable and what is truly unspeakable.

It's been swell sharing these with you. Hang tight, reader. More is coming.

Acknowledgements

None of anything I would do would be possible without the love and support of my wife, Lynda. She was very understanding and cheerleader-y on the occasions when I had to do this instead of journalism and other work. She's keen on my continued sanity for many reasons, but mostly because she loves me. This is her book.

Much love for the faith of Carmilla Voiez and SJ Davis. The two of them gave me the opportunity of a lifetime, and I'm trying really hard to live up to it for them.

I think of all the people who have told me they wanted to see this collection exist, and it was Karmin Dahl who made the biggest difference. Her constant encouragement and demand that I bring this to her was sometimes the only thing that got words in the document. Thanks, Dahl.

Lastly, there's Dori, sweet, wonderful Dori who saw past my fanboy crush to join this journey with me. I'm too much of a coward to tread water without a partner, and I am honored beyond all measure that she agreed to bring my characters to visual life. There ain't another one like her anywhere in the world.

And to all my fans, stop calling yourselves that. It's weird and awkward. We're friends. Alright? Just friends, and for that, I'm thankful.

Jef Rouner, 02/21/2015

I am honored to work with the brilliant Jef and very thrilled that he chose me to illustrate his amazing stories. I can only hope our union continues on through many more projects.

Dori Hartley, 02/22/2015

Jef Rouner (Previously known as Jef With One F) is an award-winning journalist and musician. He spends most of his days writing articles on pop culture and social justice for the *Houston Press* and *Cracked*, squeezing in a tale here or a song there with his partner Bill Curtner in The Ghost of Cliff Burton. He currently resides in Houston with his wife and daughter.

Dori Hartley is an illustrator and a portrait artist whose work can be found in many publications, as well as in hundreds of homes around the world. She is a graduate of Parsons The New School For Design, The Art Institute and The Finishing School. She has illustrated several children's books. *The Rook Circle* is Hartley's first adult novel.

Made in the USA
San Bernardino, CA
10 March 2016